P9-DBT-013

Geronimo Stilton

Scholastic Inc.

Published by Scholastic Inc., 557 Broadway, New York, NY 10012. SCHOLASTIC and associated logos are trademarks and/or registered trademarks of Scholastic Inc.

ISBN 978-0-545-83536-7

Text by Thea Stilton
Original title *Il segreto delle Fate delle Nuvole*
Cover by Flavio Ferron
Illustrations by Danilo Barozzi, Chiara Balleello, and Barbara Pellizzari (design), and Alessandro Muscillo (color)
Graphics by Marta Lorini

Special thanks to Tracey West
Translated by Emily Clement
Interior design by Becky James

12 11 10 9 8 7 6 5 4 3 2 1 15 16 17 18 19/0

Printed in Singapore 46

First edition 2015

Thea Stilton and the Thea Sisters
THEA
PAULINA
Colette
Violet
nicky
PAMELA

The Land of Clouds

High up, suspended in the clouds, there is an enchanted fantasy world where everything is light and colorful. It is the Land of Clouds, where beautiful fairies and mythical creatures live, ruled by Queen Nephele.

Queen Nephele lives in the Cloud Castle and rules over the Land of Clouds with great wisdom. Her subjects love her for this, and for her kindness.

Galatea is a member of the Grand Council of Fairies and is best friends with Ariette.

Ariette is one of the Weaver Fairies, who weave the strands that make up the clouds. She also knows how to read the dreams of other fairies while they sleep!

The Hundred-Handed Giant was cursed by a spell and must always keep his hundred hands busy.

The Color Pixies love to play tricks. They live in Fairywing Village and are also great cooks!

Airavata is an elephant with seven trunks who guards the passage into the Land of Clouds.

The Wind Elves are as light as feathers. They blow the winds that move the clouds in the sky, and they live in the Windy Cave.

Sleep Fairies are sweet, kind creatures who watch over sleep in the Land of Clouds. They live in Sleep Flower Woods.

King Nebus rules the Kingdom of Nimbus and is a just and courageous leader. He is secretly in love with Queen Nephele.

The Scarlet Lightning Fairies live in the Valley of Infinite Storm Clouds and have the most explosive personalities in the Land of Clouds!

SUMMER IS HERE!

SUMMER was in the air at Mouseford Academy. The students chattered excitedly in the hallways, happy that it was almost time for vacation. The Thea Sisters walked out into the school courtyard after their last MARINE BIOLOGY class.

"I really liked learning about tropical fish," Violet was saying. "I would love to paint pictures of them during our break."

Colette got a dreamy look in her eyes. "I would love to design a dress the color of a BLUE STARFISH."

"Well, I'm thinking of doing some ocean diving around here," Nicky said.

"That's because you can't sit still," Pam teased. "Me, I think I'll try to invent a new recipe for some **SEAFOOD PIZZA**."

Paulina's long black braid swung behind her as she turned to look at Nicky. "I think diving sounds like fun, too. There are some old **shipwreck** sites out there," she said. "I've been researching the history of them. Some of them are —"

Before she could finish her sentence, someone tapped her on the shoulder. It was me, THEA STILTON!

"Hi, Thea!" my friends greeted me, **surprised**. I hadn't told them I was coming, and I wasn't teaching there that semester.

"What are you doing here?" Pam asked.

"I have something to tell you," I said. "Can you follow me into my office?"

"What's going on, Thea?" Paulina asked eagerly when we were all settled.

"I was thinking of organizing a class in fantasy languages for you, with Will Mystery from the Seven Roses Unit," I told them. "Are you interested?"

The mouselets shared a look and smiled happily.

"Yes!" they shouted together.

The **SEVEN ROSES UNIT** is an important department in a top secret research facility. The unit specializes in fantasy worlds, and the Thea Sisters and I have helped them solve several fascinating MYSTERIES.

"I know it's your break," I went on. "But I thought brushing up on fantasy languages would be a good idea. This way, if Will Mystery calls for our HELP again, we'll be ready."

"Of course!" Pam said.

"Does that mean we'll go to their headquarters?" Nicky asked. She loves to TRAVEL.

I nodded. "Yes."

Paulina happily clapped her paws. "This will be more fun than any vacation!"

Just then, there was a knock on the office door.

I opened it and found a deliverymouse there. He was tapping his foot impatiently.

"**YOU THEA STILTON?**" he asked, in a very sharp tone.

When I said yes, he didn't reply — he just had me sign a receipt, and then thrust a **SMALL PACKAGE** into my paws.

TOP SECRET COMMUNICATION

"It's from the **SEVEN ROSES UNIT**!" Paulina cried, recognizing the symbol stamped on the package.

Before I could open it, the squeal of a ringtone came from inside. I quickly opened the box and found a cell phone in it. Will Mystery's face popped up on the screen, and I pressed the speakerphone button.

"WILL! It's nice to hear from you," I said.

"You, too, Thea," he replied. "Hope you don't mind the special-delivery phone. This phone line is highly protected, and only used in an **EMERGENCY**."

"Is that why you're calling?" I asked.

"I'm afraid so," he replied. "There's a

problem in the Land of Clouds."

"The Land of Clouds?" I asked. The Thea Sisters gathered closer to the phone, anxious to know more.

"It is one of the secret fantasy worlds," he explained. "I believe that it is in danger."

"Did a new CRACK appear on the map in the Hall of the Seven Roses?" Nicky asked. The map was a MAGICAL one, and a crack meant that a fantasy land was in trouble.

"That's EXACTLY what happened," Will confirmed. "I must travel to the Land of Clouds as soon as possible."

"Do you need our help?" I asked.

Will Mystery and the Seven Roses Unit

Will Mystery

He is the head of the Seven Roses Unit, a research team that studies fantasy worlds — the worlds inhabited by characters from myths and legends.

Hidden HQ

The headquarters of the Seven Roses Unit is hidden beneath the ice of Antarctica. Only the members of the unit know how to find the entrance.

Crystal Pendants

Researchers who work for the unit receive a crystal pendant in the shape of a rose. It contains their ID and allows them to open doors throughout the headquarters.

The Magical Map and the Crystal Elevator

In the heart of the unit, inside the Hall of the Seven Roses, a magical map shows all of the fantasy worlds and their state of health. When a world is in danger, a crack appears on the map. Also in the hall is the crystal elevator, which leads directly to the fantasy worlds. Only Will Mystery can operate it.

Thea Stilton and the Thea Sisters

Thea and her students became agents of the Seven Roses Unit due to their great talent as investigators. They work undercover, and when they receive a request for help, they are always ready to lend a paw.

"Of course!" said Will. "That's why I called you. You are the PERFECT agents for this job. When can you leave?"

I looked at the Thea Sisters, who were beaming with excitement.

"*Right away!*" I replied.

Will smiled. "Great! I will send our helicopter to pick you up at SUNSET."

"We'll be ready," I promised.

The call ended and I turned to my students. Everyone's eyes shone with enthusiasm.

WE WERE READY TO SET OFF ON A NEW ADVENTURE!

FASTEN YOUR SEAT BELTS!

"READY?" I asked, standing in the doorway of Pam and Colette's room. The Thea Sisters had gathered there to finish their final packing.

"I just need to find my brush," Colette said, looking through all her drawers. "That Antarctic air can be tough on my FUR. Ah, here it is!"

We headed outside as the sun was setting. Luckily, all the other students and teachers were inside the DINING HALL for dinner, and they didn't notice us leave. That's always important when you're on a **TOP SECRET MISSION**.

"What a lovely evening," Violet said, looking at the pink-tinged sky.

We hurried to the heliport down by the docks.

"There it is!" Paulina cried, pointing upward.

A helicopter rapidly descended toward us without making a sound. When it landed, we saw the symbol of the Seven Roses Unit on its side.

The door of the aircraft opened, and the pilot signaled for us to board.

"I'm Agent 927," he said. "Welcome!"

I sat next to him. "Thank you, Agent. This is a very quiet helicopter."

"It's an E-67 Ultrasonic," he informed me. "It's as quiet as a RAT sneaking through a CAT convention."

Oooh!
Here's the helicopter!

Pam laughed. "That's pretty quiet."

We all took our seats.

"FASTEN YOUR SEAT BELTS!" the pilot ordered.

We obeyed, and seconds later the helicopter rose up as silently as a leaf lifted by the WIND.

Below us, the lights of Mouseford Academy turned on one by one. Soon, our beloved island became just a tiny dot in the middle of the sea.

OUR ADVENTURE HAD BEGUN!

INTO THE ICEBERG

Before we knew it, we could see Antarctica below us.

"This helicopter is really fast," I remarked.

"The E-67 is as fast as a RAT being chased out of a CAT convention," Agent 927 said.

"I think he needs to work on some new jokes," Pam whispered to Nicky.

It was dark outside, but in the distance I could see a huge WHITE ICEBERG gleaming in the moonlight. The helicopter was flying **DANGEROUSLY CLOSE** to it!

"We're going to hit it!" cried Colette.

But our pilot just stared calmly ahead.

We moved CLOSER and CLOSER to the iceberg. I was about to grab the controls myself when Agent 927 pushed a

button . . . and a hole opened up in the iceberg!

The pilot expertly flew the helicopter into the opening, and we dropped into a **vertical tunnel**.

"**Holey cheese!**" yelled a shocked

Pam. "We're descending into the iceberg!"

We were all surprised. The Thea Sisters pressed their noses against the windows so they wouldn't miss a moment of the incredible maneuver. At the bottom of the tunnel I saw a platform with the symbol of the Seven Roses Unit on it. The helicopter landed on it, and the pilot turned off the motor.

When we stepped out of the helicopter, WILL MYSTERY was waiting for us.

"Good to see you!" I said.

"Did you have a good trip?" he asked.

I looked over at Agent 927. "It was definitely exciting!" I replied.

"That tunnel is amazing!" said Nicky. "Is it new?"

Will nodded. "It's our newest entrance. The iceberg is the perfect cover," he said.

"And what do you think of the E-67?"

Pam grinned. "It's as quiet as a RAT sneaking through a CAT convention, and just as fast," she said, and her friends laughed.

Will shook his head. "You sound like Agent 927."

"But seriously, it's quite exceptional," said Paulina. "I can't believe how quickly it got us here."

Colette nodded. "It's a shame we can't use it to travel to the fantasy worlds."

Will's smile faded. "That reminds me, we must get moving. Please follow me. There is something I need to SHOW you."

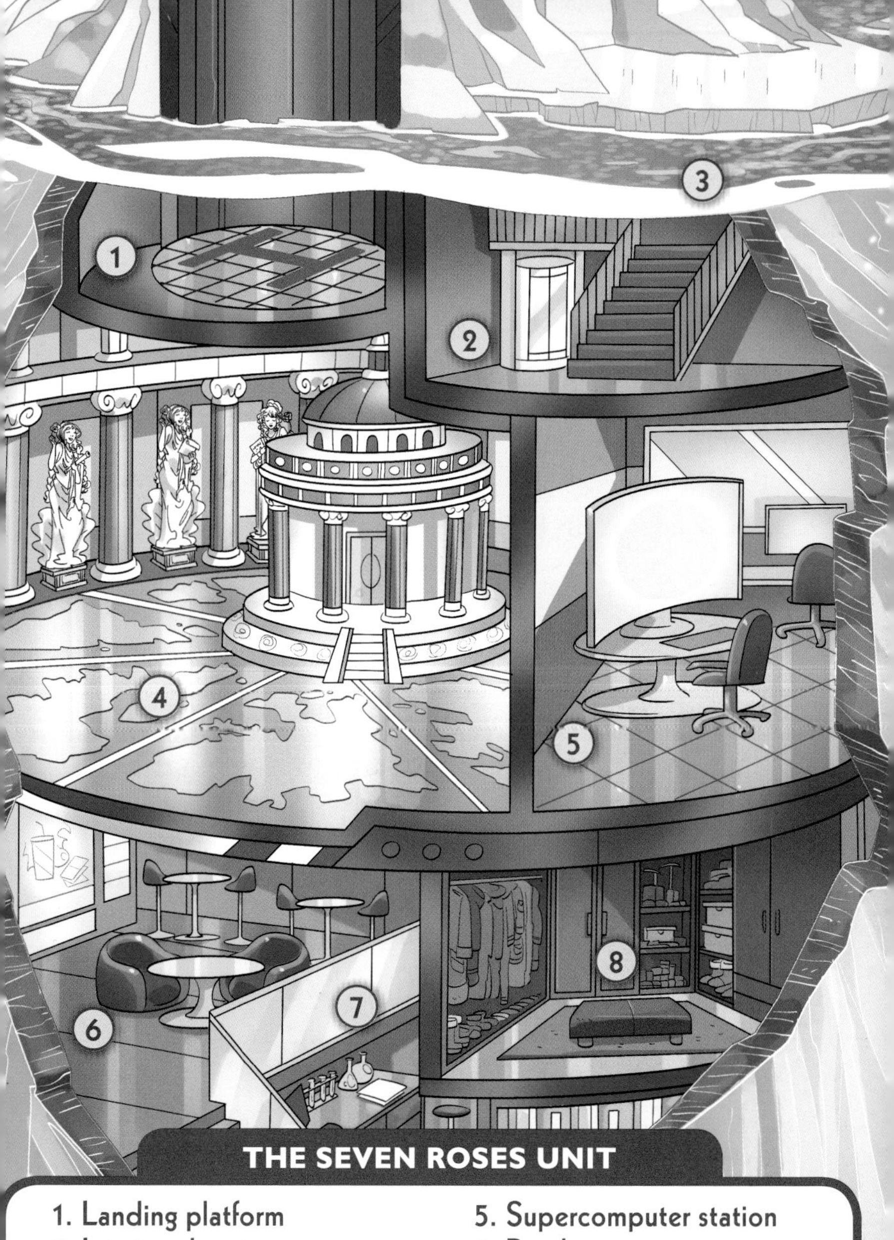

THE SEVEN ROSES UNIT

1. Landing platform
2. Interior elevator
3. Access to the iceberg
4. Hall of the Seven Roses
5. Supercomputer station
6. Break room
7. Research laboratory
8. Wardrobe storage room

NO TIME TO WASTE!

Will led us to the Hall of the Seven Roses. It has BEAUTIFUL columns, spectacular statues, and the incredible living map on the ceiling, floor, and walls.

Will used a laser pointer to show us the part of the map that depicted the Land of Clouds.

"See?" he asked in a worried voice, aiming the pointer between two blue clouds.

"There's a CRACK, just like you said," I replied.

"Yes, and unfortunately it's getting longer every day," he explained.

"A crack means that something BAD is happening there, right?" asked Nicky.

Oh no!
Look!
Hmm . . .

Will nodded. "Yes, sadly."

"That's terrible!" said Paulina.

"But we can try to help," Will said. "Let's head to the supercomputer and see what we can find out."

We left the Hall of the Seven Roses and entered a hallway with cool METAL floors and walls. Will stopped in front of a door and passed his crystal rose pendant in front of a scanner. After he said his name out loud, the door opened.

We stepped into the supercomputer station. The machine inside contained all of the information about fantasy worlds that the researchers had collected.

Will sat down at the keyboard and began to type, his paws moving SWIFTLY. Fast sequences of numbers and letters scrolled on the ENORMOUSE SCREEN in front of us.

Then Will typed in a single phrase: "Land of Clouds."

The computer gently hummed.

"This may take a while," Will said. "We've collected a lot of data over the years."

We stared at the screen, waiting for it to retrieve the information. Finally, an image appeared.

"HERE WE GO," Will said, and he began to read aloud the story of the Land of Clouds.

THE CLOUD FAIRIES

According to legend, the Cloud Fairies have lived in the sky since the start of time. There are many kinds of Cloud Fairies. One type, the Weaver Fairies, produce a silver thread when they dream at night. During the day, they use this thread to weave the clouds.

QUEEN NEPHELE

Queen Nephele rules the Land of Clouds with the assistance of the Grand Council of Fairies.

THE CLOUD CASTLE

The queen and her council dwell in the beautiful Cloud Castle. It constantly changes location because it is suspended by the air currents that crisscross the kingdom.

THE THIRTEEN-STAR DIAMOND

The entrance to the Land of Clouds will only open when thirteen stars in the sky align to form the shape of a diamond. This passageway can be found on the world's highest peak.

"We must TRAVEL to the Land of Clouds as soon as possible," Will said. "There is no time to waste."

"So let's HOP ON that crystal elevator!" Nicky said eagerly.

Will frowned. "The CRACK in the map is very deep. The elevator might be too dangerous."

"So to get there, we need to use the other entrance . . . the one on the world's HIGHEST peak," I reasoned.

Will nodded. "Exactly!"

"That's **MOUNT EVEREST**!"* Violet cried.

"Yes. With a summit at 29,035 feet, it's the **HIGHEST POINT** on Earth," Will said.

"**Cheese and crackers!** I can't even imagine being that high," said Pam.

"And I love mountain climbing, but climbing Everest is a real challenge," Nicky pointed out. "How will we do that?"

"We'll take the helicopter," said Will.

"Is it safe, at that altitude?" I asked.

"The **E-67** can do things other copters can't," Will reminded me. "But before we head out, we need more information."

* Mount Everest is part of the Himalayan mountain range and is located in Nepal. At 29,035 feet, it's the highest mountain on Earth.

A Diamond in the Sky

"Can the computer tell us exactly where the entrance to the Land of Clouds is?" Violet asked.

Will started typing on the keyboard. What popped up on the big screen SURPRISED all of us. Instead of a map with GPS coordinates, the image of a fantastical elephant appeared on the screen! It had seven trunks, and each one was a different color of the rainbow.

"How beautiful," Colette said.

"And there's a STORY that goes with it," said Paulina.

The room grew silent as we all read the story on the screen.

THE LEGEND OF THE ELEPHANT OF THE CLOUDS

The voice of the mountain tells the story of a creature gifted with extraordinary strength, but also with infinite kindness.

The winds that buffet the peaks repeat his name like a song: Airavata. He resembles an elephant with seven long trunks. With them, he sprays water into the sky and creates thick clouds. Legend says these clouds float all the way up to the stars, to the enchanted Land of Clouds.

The entrance to this magical land is located in Airavata's home: the great Diamond Rock on top of Mount Everest. The Rock shines all day and night like the brightest of stars — but only those with a watchful eye and a pure heart can spot it.

"So we need to search for a **LEGENDARY ROCK** that is hidden from plain sight," Paulina said thoughtfully.

"And don't forget," Violet added, "the entrance to the Land of Clouds only opens when thirteen stars in the sky form a diamond."

"Then let's take a telescope outside and see if we're lucky," Will said.

We all went to the wardrobe room and bundled up in jackets, scarves, and hats. We were ready for the cold of Antarctica!

Will handed a scarf to Paulina, and their paws touched briefly. They both **blushed** a little bit. Those two had admired each other since our first mission. It made sense to me, since they were both drawn to **RESEARCHING** like mice are drawn to cheese.

We all boarded the elevator to the surface of the ice.

WHOOSH! It lifted us up through headquarters. Outside, the **sky** was a dark blue storm of stars.

"It's like a beautiful painting," Violet said.

Suddenly, something bright *streaked* across the sky.

"A shooting star!" said Paulina.

"Make a wish, everyone!" Nicky said.

And so we did, in the silence of the icy polar night. It was Colette who brought us out of our thoughts.

"Should we be looking for a **DIAMOND**?" she asked.

"You're always thinking about jewelry," Pam teased.

We all laughed, including Colette.

Meanwhile, Will had set up his telescope and was **SEARCHING** the sky.

"I think I found them!" he said. "We're lucky. The thirteen stars are almost in position. Look!"

I looked through the lens of the telescope.

The stars are almost aligned!

Will was right.

"It's true. They're almost in the shape of a perfect DIAMOND," I said.

"There's no time to lose," Will said. "I'll tell Agent 927 to get the helicopter ready. We've got to get to Mount Everest and search for **Diamond Rock** before the entrance to the Land of Clouds opens!"

ON THE WORLD'S HIGHEST PEAK

We immediately went back down into headquarters and Will led us toward a storage room that contained the clothes and TOOLS needed for any kind of mission.

As we hurried down a long hallway, an agent approached Will.

"Everything's ready. The helicopter is waiting for you on the platform," she said.

Will nodded. "Thank you. We'll be there in a moment."

The agent left, and we entered the big storage room. Equipment filled the shelves that lined the walls. Racks held clothes suitable for any kind of climate, from

EXTREME HEAT to extreme cold.

"Great chunks of cheddar!" said Pam. "There's so much cool stuff here. This is better than an all-you-can-eat cheese buffet. Well, almost."

Will laughed. "We'll need some MOUNTAIN-CLIMBING gear and some OXYGEN masks," he said, pulling equipment from the shelves. "The unit has made some great advances in technology."

I was a little bit worried. "Will, summiting Everest is a challenge for seasoned mountain climbers. I'm not sure we'll be able to do this."

"Seasoned mountain climbers don't have the unit's special equipment," Will replied. "It will give us a real ADVANTAGE."

I nodded. "That makes me feel better."

"I have faith in all of you," Will said.

"But if any of you feel like you're **struggling**, let me know immediately."

"*We promise!*" the Thea Sisters all said.

Once all the gear was packed up, we headed back to the **helicopter** and got on board.

Our new **MISSION** was beginning!

As quietly as before, the helicopter

ascended the tunnel and flew up into the night sky. Then we began our IMPOSSIBLY FAST journey north and east to Nepal.

Before we knew it, Will was pointing out the snow-capped peak of Mount Everest, silhouetted against the pink morning sky.

"There it is," he said.

"It's truly majestic," I said admiringly.

"I reminds me of the Andes, back home in Peru," Paulina said. "Even though the mountains there aren't as high."

"Who knows? Maybe we'll have an adventure there one day," Will said, and Paulina smiled.

"Where should I land?" Agent 927 asked.

Will leaned forward, trying to spot Diamond Rock.

"I think I see something sparkling over there," he said. "Can we get closer?"

What a breathtaking view!

The **PILOT** kept the copter steady as he flew toward the GLITTERING snow.

"Whatever is down there, it's shining like a star, just like the computer said," Will remarked.

"And it can only be seen by a watchful EYE and a pure heart," Paulina reminded him.

"I think maybe it can only be seen if you know to LOOK for it," I reasoned.

"Hold on!" Agent 927 cried suddenly. "We've got ***HEAVY WINDS***!"

DANGER AT HIGH ALTITUDE!

We held on to our seats as the wind shook the helicopter.

"I can't land here," the pilot reported. "But I can try a little farther down the peak. You'll have to HIKE up."

We all agreed that was the safest thing to do. We landed, and an icy wind blasted us as we stepped out onto the mountain.

"Strange," Will said, looking around. "There are clouds up by the peak, but everywhere else the sky is BLUE."

We followed his gaze. He was right.

"It's so beautiful, but I've never been so cold!" Colette remarked. "Luckily, I have my **cocoa-butter-and-honey lip balm**, perfect for the coldest climates. It comes in twelve shades of pink. I'm thinking that antique rose might complement the high-altitude sky the most, don't you?"

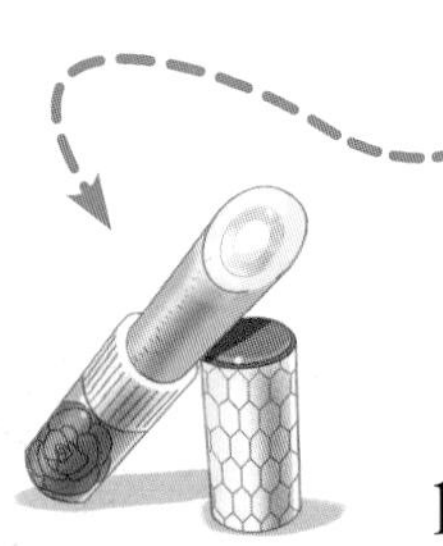

We all laughed, and Pam took a small, round tin from her pocket.

"I brought some **SHEA BUTTER**," she said. "It might not be pink, but it's great at protecting your lips from the cold."

Will took some. "Thanks, Pam!" he said. "Now, let's get going before we **freeze**!"

He opened his pack and handed each of us an **ICE HAMMER** to help with the steep climb. Then we headed toward the peak in single file, with Will at the lead. The wind blasted us with every step we took. These were the most **EXTREME** conditions I had ever experienced!

We didn't get far before Will stopped us and took out the **oxygen masks** that he had showed us before.

"At this altitude, BREATHING becomes more difficult, because the higher you climb, the less oxygen there is in the air," he explained. "But Seven Roses Unit scientists have developed these supercompact oxygen masks. Put these on and you'll see how much easier it is to breathe."

We quickly put on the **masks**, and I could immediately feel a difference.

"We can't stop here for long," I said. "We'll

risk **freezing** if we do."

Will checked to make sure our masks were on correctly, and we were on our way. In the distance, we could all see Diamond Rock shining like a **BRIGHT STAR**.

We hiked toward it, our mountain-climbing boots crunching the snow.

We had to cross a vast stretch of WHITENESS. It was difficult to even tell how far we had to go. No one spoke for a while.

Suddenly, we heard a shout.

"HEEEEEEEEEEELP!"

It was Paulina. The ice had opened up beneath her, and she was slipping into a crevasse — a break in the ice. This one was just a few feet wide.

We all watched helplessly as Paulina was swallowed by the crevasse.

"Paulina!" Nicky yelled, rushing toward the CRACK. But Will held her back.

"It's DANGEROUS," he said. "We have to do this slowly and carefully." He took a strong, thin climbing rope from his pack.

I slowly inched my way toward the crevasse.

"Paulina? Are you hurt?" I called down.

"No, but I can't climb out!" she replied.

"I'll climb down and get her," Nicky offered right away. I could see how badly she wanted to help her friend.

Will nodded. "Okay. But go slowly, all right?"

Nicky agreed, and Will harnessed the rope to her. He tied the other end around a LARGE ROCK.

"Hold on tightly as you descend," he told Nicky. "We'll keep the rope STEADY up here."

Nicky nodded, and then slowly but confidently used the rope to climb down into the crevasse. We all held our breath.

Would Nicky be able to save Paulina?

Hold steady!
I'm coming!
Nicky!

THE ICE CAVE

"*Here they come!*" Colette cried as she, Will, Pam, Violet, and I pulled on the rope with all our strength. Paulina climbed out of the crevasse first, followed by Nicky.

"I'm so glad you're **safe and sound**!" I said.

There were **hugs** all around. We were all relieved that no one had been hurt. That fall could have happened to any of us.

"**Diamond Rock** isn't far ahead," Will said, pointing, and we continued our journey.

After what had happened to Paulina, we watched the ice

with each step we took. Snowflakes started to swirl around us, making it even more difficult to move forward.

"I can't feel my legs anymore," Violet confessed.

"You said it, Vi," Colette agreed. "And I am going to need a ton of FUR CONDITIONER once we get out of this wind!"

"Maybe they serve PIZZA at Diamond Rock," Pam said hopefully.

Nicky shook her head. "Really, Pam?"

"Hey, an elephant's got to eat, right?" Pam asked. "Even a mythical one."

"Now that you mention it, how can we be sure that Airavata really lives there?" Colette asked. "He could just be a legend."

"In the Seven Roses Unit, we have learned that most legends are based on truth," Will said.

Just then, I thought I heard a **sound**.

"Did you hear that?" I asked.

Pam shook her head. "No. What did it sound like?"

"Like the ringing of a **bell**, or something similar," I replied.

"Maybe it was just the **wind**," Nicky suggested.

Finally, the **glittering** structure that we thought must be Diamond Rock was within reach. We climbed up one last ***steep incline***, and then we were standing in front of it.

"**Holey cheese!**" Pam exclaimed.

"I have never seen anything like this," Will said, his voice filled with wonder.

Diamond Rock shimmered before us. It seemed like it was made of ice, but a closer look revealed that the shine came from bright crystals. There was a big hole in the rock, like the mouth of a cave.

We hurried to take **REFUGE** inside. Once again, I swore I heard the sound of **bells**.

"Thea, I hear the **bells**, too," Will said before I could even open my mouth.

"There must be someone inside the cave," Paulina guessed.

"It could be Airavata himself!" Nicky said, her eyes GLEAMING with excitement.

Violet looked thoughtful. "The computer didn't say anything about bells, though."

Will started handing out flashlights. "We've come this far. Let's keep going."

We slowly made our way into the CAVE — and soon found that the path was blocked by a wall of ice.

"It looks like a frozen waterfall," Colette remarked.

Will and I approached the wall, studying it.

"It's not a SOLID wall," I said. "There are thin openings between the frozen waves of water, see?"

Will nodded. "I think I can get through this one."

He took off his backpack and slipped through the opening.

A few seconds later, he stuck his head out. "The passage continues. Let's keep MOVING."

We squeezed through the NARROW opening one by one and made our way through the passageway beyond it. The crystal walls gleamed every time our flashlights hit them.

"It reminds me of a fairy-tale illustration,"

Violet said, looking around wide-eyed.

The farther we went, the warmer it became in the cave. It was so odd. It felt like spring!

"Let's take off our climbing gear," suggested Will. "We'll be able to move more quickly without it."

We stashed our gear behind a ROCK and made our way farther down the passageway. Soon, we heard the sound of bells once again. Now, they were closer.

The passage opened up into what looked like a GRAND AMPHITHEATER.

"This place is amazing!" Pam said, spinning around in wonder.

JINGLE! JINGLE!

"My fur is standing on end with excitement," said Colette, shivering a little. "I have such a strange feeling — like we're about to encounter something wonderful."

"I'm feeling it, too," Paulina said, and the rest of us nodded in agreement.

I pointed my flashlight ahead of us.

"Look — stairs!" I said.

I shone my flashlight up the steps. At the top was a platform . . . and what we saw on the platform made us gasp in wonder.

An enormouse elephant stood up there. He had seven trunks, one in each color of the rainbow. Around his legs he wore GOLD BRACELETS decorated with tiny bells that rang with each step. He moved slowly, swaying as if he were dancing.

And he was heading right for us!

Look!
Oooh!
Wow!
Airavata!

AIRAVATA, THE ENCHANTED ELEPHANT

"Lower your flashlights," I said, worried that the light might be bothering the elephant. Our eyes took a moment to get used to the SHADOWY DARKNESS.

The creature moved closer to us, accompanied by the JANGLING of bells. He was **huge** and **STRONG**, but I sensed a gentleness about him.

"I am Airavata, master of this mountain, and of the winds, the snow, and the clouds here. Who are you?" he demanded in a deep voice.

Will took a step forward. "My name is Will Mystery and I am a researcher. This is my team."

"What are you looking for here?"

"We study fantasy worlds," Will replied. "And we are here because we are trying to reach the Land of Clouds."

The elephant's EYES widened. Then he was silent.

"Please excuse us for entering your CAVE without your permission. We did not mean to disturb you," Violet said. "But we know that you are the only one who can point out the secret passage to the Land of Clouds."

The elephant's yellow trunk reached for Violet and sniffed around her. I could see that she was a little afraid, but she stayed still.

Then the elephant did the same with all of us. Finally, he pulled back his trunk.

"You all have pure hearts, and you are

telling the truth," he announced. "Now explain to me why you want to go up there, among the silver clouds."

"The Land of Clouds is in DANGER," Paulina explained. "We believe that something very SERIOUS is happening there."

Airavata didn't seem surprised to hear this. He shook his large head, and his seven trunks waved from side to side.

"I don't know how you found out, but you are right," he revealed. "For some time, the fairies have no longer been weaving clouds. I am the only one who creates them now, so at least it will snow on the mountain."

"Then this must be the danger that is threatening the Land of Clouds," Paulina realized. "If the fairies aren't weaving any more clouds, sooner or later their entire world is in danger of disappearing, right?"

"I'm afraid so," Airavata replied sadly.

"We must find out why this is happening," said Colette.

"Can you please help us?" Pam asked the elephant.

He nodded. "Very well. I will help you. Follow me."

He took us down a passageway that led **deep** into the mountain — but somehow emerged outside on a ledge, with **blue sky** above us!

Airavata pointed his seven

trunks toward the sky and began to blow, shooting out sprays of water. Once the water drops hit the cold air they became tiny crystals. The crystals began to form a large, marvelous cloud.

We gazed at the scene before us, astonished.

"But where do you get the water to spray?" asked Nicky.

"I suck it up from a secret lake in the mountain," Airavata replied.

He shot another spray of water into the sky, creating a huge bank of clouds. Then he looked at us.

"Very well, my friends. The road to the Land of Clouds is open!" he announced.

"But how do we get there?" Will asked.

"It's very simple," Airavata replied. "You must climb the clouds and follow the path that I have created for you."

AIRAVATA'S POETRY

"I will help you start," Airavata said. He reached out a **trunk** toward Will and grabbed him around the waist with it, then LIFTED him onto the clouds.

But as soon as Will's feet hit the **clouds**, he began to **sink** through them. Airavata quickly brought him back down to the ledge.

"It didn't work!" Will said, disappointed.

"**I'll try!**" Colette offered.

Airavata picked her

up with a trunk and set her down on the clouds. But even she couldn't manage to stand on them for more than a few seconds.

"Why can't Will or Colette stand on the clouds?" I asked.

"Only the light can walk on the clouds," Airavata replied.

"But I'm in great shape!" Colette protested.

"I am speaking of lightness of the heart and soul," the elephant explained. "You have pure hearts, so you should be able to do it. But something is holding you back."

"What can we do?" asked Paulina.

"You must believe in your deepest wishes and your most secret dreams," Airavata said. "Only then will you be light enough to stand on the clouds."

"But we do believe in our dreams," Violet said confidently.

"Maybe not always," the elephant said wisely. "It is normal to have doubts. But you must believe that anything is possible, even when things look bleak. Only then will your heart be free to carry you above it all, to take you where dreams are born."

"Those are beautiful words," I said.

Airavata smiled. "Now, listen," he began, and then he recited a POEM. As he spoke, his words were spelled out in silver threads in the clouds overhead.

"That is a wonderful poem," Colette said.

"Repeat it to yourself when you land on the clouds," Airavata said. "It will make you feel free and light, so you won't sink."

We read the poem written overhead, trying to remember the words. Then, one by one, Airavata lifted us onto the clouds.

Your journey starts
on solid ground.
First take a leap.
You're skyward bound!

Your dreams await you
high in the sky.
If you have a pure heart,
then you shall fly.

Spread your wings.
Let your heart lead the way.
Forget your troubles.
Shine your love like a ray.

When you tread the clouds,
keep your steps light as air.
Stay on the path.
Keep your mind free from care.

I repeated the poem in my mind, and I think everyone else did, too. This time, we didn't **sink**!

We all looked at our feet, squeakless. We were standing on a soft, wispy layer of clouds!

"We're walking on clouds!" exclaimed a surprised Paulina.

"Thank you!" we all told the elephant.

He responded with a **POWERFUL TRUMPETING**. We waved good-bye, and then began to climb the cloud pathway he had created for us.

Are you ready?
Yes!
Yes!
Yes!
Yes!
Yes!
Yes!

THE SILVER GATE

"Is that a **SIGN** up ahead?" Paulina asked, pointing.

"It is!" Colette said happily as we got closer. "It's pointing the way to the Land of Clouds!"

"We must be close," said Violet, and she shivered with excitement. "I wonder what we will find there!"

Nicky was at the rear of the line. She looked behind her, and suddenly cried out.

"The clouds

behind us are disappearing!"

"Then we'd better get MOVING," I said.

We picked up our pace toward the sign along the path of fluffy clouds.

I cast a glance behind me. It made me a little nervous to see the clouds vanishing.

"Is there another SIGN up there?" Colette asked anxiously.

Then Will spotted something. "Not a sign, but I see something else. Look!"

Just ahead, we could see a tall SILVER GATE attached to two columns. It shone like a piece of jewelry and was decorated with birds on top of the posts.

We approached the gate, admiring its beauty.

"This must be the entrance," Will said.

"But it's locked, and we don't have a key," Paulina pointed out.

Look!
There it is!
Are we there?

Nicky gave the doors a PUSH, but they didn't budge.

"Now what?" Violet asked.

"Where there's a gate, there must be a gatekeeper," I said. Then I called out, "Hello! Is anyone there? Can you please open the gate for us?"

I got no reply at first. Then, amazingly, the two columns holding up the gate began to spin around. And a winged creature flew out of each column!

THE FAIRY GUARDIANS

The two winged creatures stared at us with icy blue eyes. They looked like fairies of some kind, with long blue hair that sparkled. Each one had a thin gold crown around her forehead.

Before any of us could speak, one of them grasped a small HARP that was attached to a gold chain around her neck. She started to play a sweet **melody** with low, serious tones. Then the second fairy grasped her harp and began to play in harmony with the first.

"Should we say something to them?" Colette whispered.

"It would be rude to interrupt them while they are playing," Paulina said. "We should wait until they are done."

We listened for a few more minutes, but the fairies showed no sign of ending their song.

"Hmm," said Will thoughtfully. "Maybe they are trying to communicate through music."

I nodded. "I think you're right. The music might be their language. By playing, they are trying to tell us something."

Paulina looked excited. "That makes sense! The crystal elevator in the Seven Roses Unit responds to musical commands."

"But what are they saying?" Colette asked.

"I have no idea," I admitted.

I noticed that Will was rummaging through his backpack.

"Now, **WHERE IS IT**?" he was muttering.

After a few moments of searching, he pulled a **YELLOW** instrument from the backpack — a recorder. We all watched him **curiously** as he brought the recorder to his lips.

Will began to play a tune. It was a **melody** all his own, but it perfectly matched the tune being played by the two fairies. The sweet tones of the recorder melded with the clean tones of the two harps. The sound was truly beautiful!

"I wish I had my VIOLIN with me," Violet said wistfully. "I would join in!"

We stood there listening, enchanted, until suddenly the two fairies stopped playing. They let go of their harps and listened carefully to Will play his recorder. Then they whispered to each other, smiling.

As if by magic, the silver gate slowly opened!

Will stopped playing his recorder. "**WE DID IT!**" he cheered.

"Well done, Will," I said. "It's a good thing you had that recorder with you."

"MUSIC is very important in fantasy lands, so I always bring an instrument with me," Will said. "A good agent is ALWAYS PREPARED."

"And how did you know what to play?" Violet asked.

"I simply tried to meld with the music the fairies were playing," Will explained. "After the first few notes, the tune just came flowing through me."

"It sounded beautiful," Paulina said.

"It did," Colette agreed. "But maybe we should GO through the gates before these two lovely fairies change their minds."

She pointed to them, and they both looked at us with very SERIOUS expressions.

"Good thinking, Colette," Pam said.

We quickly passed through the gates, smiling and nodding politely at the fairies.

"Thank you," I said.

Then, to my surprise, they began to speak.

"We are the Fairy Guardians of the Land of Clouds," they sang together. "Welcome! It is a pleasure to have friends of music visit our world."

"And it is an HONOR for us to visit," Will said. "Thank you for opening the silver gates for us."

"Yes, thank you," the THEA SISTERS said.

The fairies smiled back at us, and we were all struck by their beauty. Then, without another word, each one slipped back inside her COLUMN, leaving us alone.

"It was very nice of them to let us in," Colette said, "but I wish they hadn't left so quickly. I had a million questions for them!"

Will nodded. "Yes, I would have liked to ask for directions to the CLOUD CASTLE."

"That would have been nice," I agreed. "But somehow we always manage to find our way to where we need to go."

Violet nodded. "Things can be very magical in these fantasy lands."

All we could see ahead of us was an enormouse expanse of clouds.

"They look like whipped cream," Pam remarked.

We looked around, enchanted, as the silver gates closed behind us.

THE RIDDLES OF THE WIND ELVES

"How do we know where to go?" Paulina wondered. "There is no CLEAR path."

"Maybe we'll find another SIGN," Colette suggested.

So we started walking straight ahead.

"It's like we're walking on cotton

candy," Pam remarked.

"First whipped cream, now cotton candy. You must be hungry, Pam!" Nicky said.

"Come on, Nicky," Pam said. "You know that I'm *always* hungry!"

We all laughed, and kept walking. Soon a strong GUST OF WIND chilled our fur, and gray clouds appeared in the sky.

"Look!" Paulina said, amazed. "There are tiny winged creatures up there!"

She was right. The strange beings were aiming GOLD TRUMPETS at the clouds and blowing into them.

"Hello!" I called out. They didn't notice.

"Maybe music is their language, too," Violet guessed.

"I don't think so," said Will. "Their trumpets aren't making any sound. But maybe we can get their attention another way. Follow my lead."

Will took a **deep breath**, then blew hard toward the clouds. We all did the same.

The winged creatures stopped blowing into their trumpets and **STARED** at us, annoyed.

"**5+2** dare disturb the work of the Wind

Elves!" one exclaimed.

"**2 x 3 + 1** clouds they must move!" said another.

"**12 ÷ 4** times will the Wind Elves blow them away!" threatened a third elf.

You must solve our math riddles!

"**NO! WAIT!**" Will interrupted them. "Excuse us, please. We didn't mean to **disturb** you. We are trying to reach the Cloud Castle. Can you help us?"

"**3 x 3 - 7** math riddles of the Wind Elves must you solve first," a fourth elf said.

Paulina understood right away. "So we have to solve two **MATH RIDDLES**?"

"Correct," the elf replied, and the four elves huddled together, whispering. Then the first one spoke:

The second elf took an hourglass full of colorful crystals out of his pocket. He turned it over and began to count down as the crystals fell, one by one. "30... 29... 28 ..."

We all concentrated on finding the answer.

"10 clouds!" Paulina suddenly cried.

The elves were SURPRISED. Only 17 crystals had fallen through the hourglass. One elf cried, "Exactly! And 10+3 crystals remain. Congratulations!"

"Good job, Paulina!" we cheered.

But the elves soon had a second math riddle for us.

"Listen closely, and please think.
There are 3 blue clouds and 2 pink.
Each blue cloud has 2 drops of rain.
Each pink cloud has 3 drops of rain.
How many drops of rain are in the sky?
You have 30 seconds to reply!"

The same elf turned over the hourglass.

"You could have given us some warning," Colette muttered as we all tried to solve the math riddle.

This time, I had the answer first.

"12!" I cried, after only a few CRYSTALS had fallen.

We looked at the elf, waiting to see if I was correct.

"Correct," he said. "You have been very clever. Now you will receive the answer you seek."

"HOORAY!" we cheered.

"Thank you," said Will. "Can you please tell us how to get to the Cloud Castle?"

"It's difficult to say," the first elf replied. "The Cloud Castle is ALWAYS MOVING.

If you like, one of us could stay with you as your guide."

"Thank you! You are very kind,"

Violet said.

Without another word, the Wind Elves positioned themselves behind the clouds and began to blow.

One of them waved good-bye to the others and blew his little cloud toward us. He settled right over our heads, as if he was waiting for a COMMAND.

"Well now, what do we do?" Nicky asked, looking up at the elf. But the elf said nothing.

"Maybe we should start WALKING," Colette suggested, and she took a few steps forward. As she moved, the elf moved, too.

"It looks like he's coming with us," Paulina said.

The elf quickly took the lead. We followed him as he continued to push his **little cloud** forward with his trumpet.

THE ENCHANTED WOODS

The elf led us to another signpost in the clouds.

"The Enchanted Woods," I read aloud.

"That name sounds a little **spooky**," Colette said with a shiver.

"Well, the elf seems to think it's the way to go," I said, looking up at him.

So we followed the sign to a staircase made of **clouds**. It led us to a forest — and the **trees** were made of clouds, too!

"It's like something from a fairy tale," Violet said.

"Yes, but let's hope a **WICKED WITCH** doesn't live here," said Pam.

We walked toward the strange, **fluffy** trees. Everything was cloaked in a strange silence. Then, Colette suddenly let out a cry.

"**NOOOOO!**" she wailed.

"Heeeeeelp!" yelled Violet.

I rushed over to them, but before I could reach them, I stopped, **confused**.

The fluffy trees around me had disappeared. Instead, I was back in the **GARDEN AT MOUSEFORD ACADEMY**!

I froze, shocked. How could I have gotten there? And it looked **different** from how I remembered it. The buildings were **CRACKED** and there were no students in sight.

Then an **OLD RODENT** slowly walked toward me, leaning on a cane.

"Professor de Mousus!" I said, recognizing the academy's headmaster. My heart was beating **quickly**. "What is going on?"

But the headmaster didn't reply. He just shook his head with a **sad** look on his face.

"Thea! Thea!" I heard a voice, and someone touched my arm.

I woke up, as if from a **dream**, and saw Will standing next to me.

"Help me, Will!" I said. "We must help

Professor de Mousus!"

"No, Thea, the professor is not here," Will said.

"Yes, he is!" I insisted. "But he's old, and the academy is in RUINS, and he needs our help!"

"It's just an ILLUSION, Thea," Will told me.

"You are seeing your fears come true. It's a trick of the Enchanted Woods."

"What?" I asked. I was seeing the professor with my own EYES! "I don't understand. How can this be an illusion?"

"The clouds here take the form of the fears of those who pass," he replied.

"But why aren't you seeing anything frightening?" I asked.

"I've been taking a course dedicated to learning how to control my emotions," Will explained. "Try to concentrate, Thea."

I closed my eyes and opened them again. But I could still see the abandoned academy and Professor de Mousus.

"Wait here for a moment," Will said. He rushed off and brought all the Thea Sisters over. Each of them was terrified by the vision of her own fears, too.

"Thea, I'm so **scared**," Violet said, reaching out to grab my paw.

"You must think of positive things," Will told us. "Think of your **friendship**."

That gave Colette an idea. She reached into her pocket and pulled out her phone. Then she scrolled down the screen and pulled up a **photo**.

"**That's us!**" Nicky cried. "It was right

after we finished our finals at the end of last semester."

I was in the photo, too, and the happy memory came flooding back to me. The Thea Sisters had all done well on their tests and were excited about the vacation coming up.

When I looked up from the photo, I saw that my vision of the academy had vanished! I was back in the cloud forest. The others were looking around, wide-eyed.

"Everything's back to normal," Paulina said.

Nicky grinned. "All our fears have vanished!"

"Colette's photo defeated them," added Pam.

Will smiled. "Actually, what made your fears disappear was your friendship!"

A FAIRY IN DANGER

As soon as we took a few steps, the Enchanted Woods vanished behind us. But now we had another problem. Our Wind Elf and his little cloud had also disappeared. We had lost our guide!

"Now what do we do?" Pam asked as we looked around. The landscape had completely transformed. Now we were standing on a large platform of clouds that extended as far as the eye could see in every direction. There was no clear path to take.

"There must be a sign somewhere," Colette said, but there was nothing on the HORIZON except for more clouds.

"**WAIT!** Can you hear that?" Paulina asked.

We all listened closely.

"It sounds like someone is crying," I said.

"But where is it coming from?" Will asked.

Nicky concentrated. "I'm not sure, but it

sounds like a female voice."

"Whoever is crying is very **sad**," Colette observed. "We must help her!"

But we had to **FIND** her before we could help her.

"Let's keep walking forward," I suggested.

As we moved on, the **CRYING** seemed to get louder.

"I think we're on the right track," Paulina said hopefully.

Then, suddenly, the crying just **STOPPED**.

"Is somebody there?" Colette called out. "Do you need our help?"

But NOBODY answered her.

We looked at one another, discouraged. Just as we thought we were getting close, our JOURNEY had ended. Or had it?

"LOOK! Straight ahead!" Pam cried, pointing.

"It's a tower!" Paulina said. "A TOWER OF CLOUDS!"

The tall blue tower rose from the clouds in the far distance.

"It must be very tall, if we can see it from here," Will reasoned.

"Shhh!" Paulina interrupted. "I hear the crying again."

We hurried toward the tower, and the crying got louder with each step we took. It was very clear that the crying and the tower were connected. But how?

When we arrived at the tower, we realized that Will's guess was correct. The tower was impossibly high. And there didn't seem to be a door at the bottom, just a window all the way at the top.

We were searching the base of the tower for some kind of entrance when DROPS started falling from above. Nicky collected one in her paw and sniffed it.

"It smells like salt water," she said. "Wait, could these be tears?"

"Oh no!" said Colette. "The poor, sad soul is TRAPPED in the top of the tower! We must find a way inside."

"Let's circle the tower and see if we're missing something," Will suggested.

We walked around the whole base of the building, feeling it with our paws, but we could not find an ENTRANCE.

"Hmm. Maybe the entrance is under the clouds somewhere," I guessed.

Will looked up. "Well, we know for sure that the WINDOW is a way in. Here's what I'm thinking. Let's split up. I will climb the tower with Colette, Paulina, and Pam."

I nodded. "And Nicky, Violet, and I will see what we can find beneath the clouds."

Will still had some ropes and climbing gear in his backpack. While Violet, Nicky, and I searched through the clouds for some way into the tower, Will and the others prepared for the climb.

SURPRISINGLY, climbing the tower was easier than they thought. The clouds were strangely firm and allowed them to grip with their paws and shoes as they climbed.

Will cheered on his team. "You're doing

great! We're halfway there!"

"I'm so curious to see who is inside," Colette admitted.

Down below, we couldn't find a way in.

"There aren't any **TRAPDOORS**," Violet reported.

Nicky looked up.

"I hope they have better luck than we're having!"

I followed her gaze. Will, Colette, Pam, and Paulina had REACHED the window!

Will told me later exactly what happened when they climbed inside the tower. They entered a **circular room** made of clouds: the walls, the fireplace, even the four-poster bed. The white clouds were tinged with pale yellow and blue.

In front of the fireplace stood a fairy with long red hair. She was quite beautiful, but she had the saddest look on her face. Will and the others were certain: they had found the crying creature!

Oooh!
Oh!

THE STORY OF ARIETTE

Will, Colette, Pam, and Paulina did not speak for a few moments. They stared at the fairy in the tower room, enchanted by her beauty and sadness.

She was the one who spoke first.

"I am happy to see you, strangers," she said in a voice that was as sweet as the sound of a flute or the song of a spring bird.

"We heard your cries, and we couldn't ignore them," Will said gallantly.

"Yes," said Colette. "We want to help you."

The fairy nodded. "You were very courageous to climb all the way up here."

Then she gave a little bow. "I should introduce myself. My name is Ariette and I am a Weaver Fairy."

"A Weaver Fairy? Does that mean you can make clouds?" asked Pam, remembering what they had learned back at the unit headquarters.

"Yes," said Ariette. "At least, I used to be able to make clouds." She sighed and sat down.

"Why can't you now? What happened?" Will asked.

"It is a very sad story," she replied. "Would you like to hear it?"

"Certainly," said Will. "Once we hear it, we can figure out how to help you."

"Thank you, you are truly kind," said Ariette. "But I don't know your names."

"Of course! I'm sorry," Will said. "My name is Will Mystery and I'm a researcher."

"And we're Colette, Pam, and Paulina," Colette said, pointing to her friends. "We're colleagues of Will's, and we go to Mouseford Academy."

"I'm afraid I've never heard of it," Ariette said.

"It's located in the REAL WORLD," Paulina explained. "Very far from here."

Ariette's eyes LIT UP. "I know of the real world," she said. "Please tell me, what do you research?"

"We study the worlds of fantasy and solve mysteries there," Will replied.

"And is that why you are here in the Land

of Clouds?" the fairy asked.

Colette nodded. "We know that the Weaver Fairies have stopped making clouds. We're here to find out what happened."

A SHADOW crossed Ariette's face. "That is why I've been locked up in this tower."

"What do you mean?" Will asked.

"Well, it is believed that the reason the Weaver Fairies don't weave anymore is that they no longer dream," Ariette replied.

Will nodded. "Yes, we read that the silver threads that make the clouds are produced when Weaver Fairies dream," he said. "But why aren't you dreaming anymore?"

"The others blame me," Ariette said sadly. "They say that I disturbed the sleep of my fairy friends by telling them about the WORLD BELOW."

"The World Below?" Paulina asked.

"That is what all Cloud Fairies call the world that exists **BELOW THE SKY** — the real world, as you call it," Ariette explained.

Pam was confused. "What did you tell the other fairies about the real world that **STOPPED** them from dreaming?"

"I told them nothing that would have disturbed their dreams," Ariette insisted. "I only told them about the many wonders of your world. But I broke our **RULE** that Weaver Fairies may never know about the World Below."

"Why not?" Colette asked.

"So that we can concentrate on our work," the fairy explained. "Weaver Fairies must only focus on weaving the clouds. And we cannot pass beyond the boundaries of the Land of Clouds."

Paulina nodded. "So you must have been

very curious about the World Below."

"Yes, very curious," Ariette said. "That's why I was punished and IMPRISONED in this tower."

"Who imprisoned you?" Will asked.

"Queen Nephele," Ariette replied. "She is very worried. If the fairies don't start weaving clouds soon, the Land of Clouds will disappear!"

Paulina frowned. "But if you are not the reason why the Weaver Fairies are not dreaming, then what is?"

"I am not sure," Ariette admitted. "But I think I know a way to FIND OUT."

"How?" Pam asked.

"I am the only fairy who can SEE the dreams of the other weavers," Ariette explained. "If I manage to find out what is really disturbing them, I'll also find out what created this situation."

"And then you could also prove your innocence!" said Colette.

"Yes, but to do that . . ." Paulina began.

"I have to get out of here!" Ariette cried.

THE CRYSTALS OF THE FAIRIES

Colette looked around. "Have you ever tried to **escape**?"

"It's not that simple," Ariette replied. "Each of the Weaver Fairies possesses a special pendant with a very BRIGHT CRYSTAL."

"That sounds beautiful," Colette remarked.

"They are quite beautiful to look at," Ariette said. "But even more beautiful is their meaning. Inside each PENDANT is a picture that represents the nature of the fairy who wears it. Mine has a picture of a heart."

"What does the heart represent?" asked Paulina.

Ariette smiled. "I am very **sensitive** to the feelings of others."

"That's an important quality," said Will.

"But what does your pendant have to do with being IMPRISONED in the tower?" Paulina asked.

"The pendant was taken away from me when I was imprisoned," Ariette explained. "I am unable to move around the Land of Clouds without it."

"Why not?" Pam asked.

"The crystal contains my spirit, the core of who I am," Ariette said. "Without my crystal, I am powerless and weak. I am just a SHADOW of the fairy I once was."

"That is so sad," said Colette. "Isn't there

anything we can do to help you?"

"Yes, there is," said Ariette. "You could help me get back my PENDANT."

Paulina was listening thoughtfully. "If Queen Nephele took it from you, is the pendant in the Cloud Castle now?"

"No, it is guarded by the Color Pixies," Ariette replied. "They're always happy and joking around, so much that it is difficult to know when they're actually being **SERIOUS**."

"So getting the pendant should be pretty easy, then," said Pam.

Ariette shook her head. "For some reason, the Color Pixies have grown very suspicious lately. They don't let anyone into their village anymore."

"We'll just tell them we're there to get your CRYSTAL," said Colette.

"They won't trust you," Ariette insisted. "And you shouldn't even mention the crystal. If you can, find out where it is and then sneak away with it."

Will was surprised. "You want us to steal it?"

Ariette sighed. "I'm afraid that is the only way. According to the queen, I am a CRIMINAL. The only way I can prove my innocence is to get the crystal back so I can travel to the Weaver Fairies and see their dreams. And that is the only way to save the Land of Clouds. You believe me, don't you?"

Will, Colette, Pam, and Paulina looked at one another. They had met other beautiful fairies before who were not so nice inside. They had no reason to trust her — but there was something special about Ariette,

You want us to
steal the crystal?

and they all felt it.

Will turned to Ariette and nodded. "Very well. We will help you."

"I am very grateful," said Ariette. "When you return with the CRYSTAL, I will help you reach the Cloud Castle. Then we can work together to solve the Mystery of the fairies' dreams."

"Where can we find the Color Pixies?" asked Pam.

"They live in Fairywing Village, a small town not far from here," Ariette replied. "To get there, you must follow the color clouds. You will know Fairywing Village as soon as you see it. The village is made of clouds in every color of the rainbow."

"How pretty!" said Colette. "But how will we get into the village if you say the pixies won't let anyone in?"

"There is one way to gain their TRUST," answered Ariette. "You must make them laugh! The Color Pixies love to laugh. If you can tell them a FUNNY JOKE, they quickly become friendly and trusting."

"That will be an interesting challenge," observed Paulina.

"I'm sure we can do it," Will said confidently.

"We should get going," said Colette. "Thea and the others will be waiting for us."

"There are more of you?" Ariette asked.

"There are seven of us all together," Paulina replied.

"Wonderful! Together you will be stronger!" the fairy said, smiling.

Then the mice said good-bye to Ariette and made their way down the tower.

THE CLOUD TUNNEL

"What a sad story. Poor Ariette," remarked Violet after Will told us the story of the tower's fairy prisoner.

"What do you think, Thea?" Will asked.

"Did she seem sincere?" I asked.

"Yes," said Will.

"Although she could have been lying to get back her CRYSTAL," added Colette.

"But we all felt there was something very truthful about her," said Pam. "And she might be the only one who can help us find out what is happening to the Weaver Fairies."

"Then we must find Fairywing Village!" I said, and we set off to find the color clouds.

Let's go!
Oh!

We looked at the clouds ahead of us as we walked.

"There's a yellow one!" Paulina said, pointing.

"And I see a blue and a pink one," added Colette.

"Let's be quick, then, before they float away!" Will said.

We stepped on the puffy clouds. It was almost like following a path of stepping-stones, except these felt like balloons under our feet.

The color clouds led us to a hill made of white, fluffy clouds.

Will frowned. "Ariette didn't mention this."

"Maybe the path continues on the other side," I guessed.

"Then let's climb over the hill," Will said.

"We already climbed up the tower. It shouldn't be too **difficult**," Paulina said, and she took the first step on the hill.

As soon as she set her foot down, the clouds turned **PURPLE** and rumbled. Then they **shoOk violently**, and Paulina toppled over.

Nicky ran to her. "Are you hurt?"

"I'm fine," Paulina replied. "Luckily, the clouds are **soft**."

The clouds making up the hill had turned white again.

"Let me try," said Will, but as soon as he began to climb, the clouds turned dark again and trembled, sending him TUMBLING backward.

"Maybe we should try going around the hill," I suggested.

We agreed that was the best thing to do. We hadn't gone far when Nicky pointed.

"Look! A **TUNNEL**!" she cried.

There was an opening in the clouds at the bottom of the hill. Near the opening was a sign.

"CLOUD TUNNEL," read Paulina. "How mysterious!"

It was extremely

foggy inside the tunnel. Will produced a flashlight from his backpack and pointed it in front of him.

"There's a footprint!" Paulina said.

"Judging by its size, it belongs to someone very BIG," Colette commented.

That very large footprint worried me, but we kept going. As we made our way through the tunnel, the fog became THINNER and THINNER. We had traveled far when we reached a large room illuminated by many candles. Shelves held hundreds of bottles filled with COLORFUL LIQUIDS.

Then we saw something move in the very back of the room . . . something large and heavy.

We all gasped as a

GIANT stepped toward us! He had so many arms that we couldn't count them!

THE HUNDRED-HANDED GIANT

The giant moved toward us, waving his many hands. Each one held a **BOTTLE** of colorful liquid.

"Who goes there?" he thundered.

"We are researchers," Will answered.

"Why have you come to my house?" the giant asked.

"We did not mean to **disturb** you," Will said. "We didn't know you lived here."

"Everyone in the land knows that!" boomed the giant. "I am the **Hundred-Handed Giant**. Where are you from?"

"From the World Below," Colette called out.

The giant looked interested.

"I was in the **WORLD BELOW** a long, long

time ago," he said.

As he spoke, we heard the sound of BREAKING GLASS. One of the bottles had broken in the giant's hand. He rushed to take another from a shelf.

"How long have you lived here?" Will asked.

"I do not know," the GIANT replied. "Here, time does not pass. And I am condemned to always keep my hands occupied. I cannot rest for a single moment."

"Is that why you're holding a bottle in every hand?" I asked.

The giant nodded. "Yes. Once, I traveled to a faraway land. I was young and arrogant then, and when I came across an ugly WITCH I laughed in her face. So she punished me by giving me a hundred hands."

"How cruel!" said Colette.

"She taught me a **lesson** that appearances do not matter, and I have learned it," said the giant.

"But why must your hands always be occupied?" Paulina wondered.

"It is part of the **curse**," said the giant sadly. "My hands must always be doing something, or I shall die. So I constantly empty and refill these bottles."

"That is awful," said Colette. "I wish we could stay and keep you company."

"Yes, but we have a very important assignment," added Will. "The Weaver Fairies are no longer making clouds. If we don't find out why this is happening, the **Land of Clouds** will disappear."

The giant frowned. "I did not know this. I never venture outside my tunnel. But if it's true that the Land of Clouds is in DANGER, then I will help you."

"Thank you," said Colette. "You are very kind."

"Kindness is another lesson I have learned," the giant said with a smile.

"Do you know the way to Fairywing Village?" asked Will.

"I can point out the road to

you, but I can't go with you," the giant said. "First you must pass through the VALLEY OF INFINITE STORM CLOUDS."

"That sounds DANGEROUS," said Pam.

"The valley is swept by very strong winds that bring storm clouds with them," the giant explained. "These clouds create the Scarlet River, which is very difficult to cross. The SCARLET LIGHTNING FAIRIES live in the river, and they do not like strangers. You must be careful."

"We will be," I promised.

The giant led us to the end of the tunnel. We said good-bye to him, and before long, we came to a valley of ANGRY RED CLOUDS. We walked to the edge and looked down into the swirling storm clouds.

IT WAS TRULY TERRIFYING!

THE SCARLET LIGHTNING FAIRIES

"Do we really have to climb down there?" Violet asked nervously, looking out over the Valley of Infinite Storm Clouds.

"I'm afraid so, if we want to reach Fairywing Village," I replied.

"How will we cross the Scarlet River?" Paulina asked, looking down at the river of clouds. "It's moving awfully quickly."

Will looked thoughtful. "Maybe there is a way to stop it. Like another RIDDLE."

"We can ask the Scarlet Lightning Fairies," Colette said.

Dressed in bright red, the SCARLET LIGHTNING FAIRIES flew above the river, sprinkling dust on the storm clouds.

Whoooosh!
That's astounding!
Hmm . . .

"They don't look friendly," Nicky remarked. "But I guess we have to try."

With a nod, Will set off down the SLOPING valley of clouds. As we followed him, the WIND became more intense.

"Hang on tight!" I called out. Just one STRONG GUST of wind could send any one of us falling into the river below!

We finally made it down to the riverbank.

Suddenly, two Scarlet Lightning Fairies swooped down from above. They looked ANGRY, but they were beautiful, and I marveled at their hair. It was deep red and WILD and wavy, like the storm clouds.

"Who are you?" asked the first fairy.

"We don't want INTRUDERS in our valley," said the second.

"We are here to help the Land of Clouds,"

I said as sweetly as I could.

"YOU MUST LEAVE," the first fairy snapped. "You cannot stay."

"Please, fairies, we just want to pass through," said Colette.

"NO!" the second fairy said firmly.

"But we are on a very important mission," Will pleaded. "We come from the World Below, and we saw that your land is in trouble. There is no time to waste!"

"We said no!" the first fairy cried.

As she spoke, a JAGGED BOLT OF LIGHTNING

fell from the sky and hit the clouds right next to us!

"Hey! Are you trying to hurt us?" Pam asked.

"That was not us!" the second fairy said with a huff. "It is the clouds. They are too **small** and weak to hold an electrical charge these days."

"It's no fun making lightning when the clouds can't hold it!" added the first fairy.

"That's why we're here," Colette said.

Then another LIGHTNING BOLT fell from the clouds. It singed the first fairy!

"**OUCH!**" she yelped.

"If you want to stop this from happening, then please let us pass," Colette continued. "The reason the clouds are **small** and weak is that the Weaver Fairies aren't producing any new ones!"

"What would you know about the Land of Clouds?" the second fairy asked with a scoff.

"We research fantasy worlds, and we think we know how to help," said Will.

But the fairies just shook their heads. The first fairy raised her arms to the sky. Immediately, a *GUST OF WIND* blew down and she shaped it in her hands.

We watched, amazed, as the wind in the fairy's hands became a sphere. It grew **BIGGER** and **BIGGER**. Once it was the size of a large cheese ball, she got ready to throw it at us.

"Go away!" she shouted.

Just then, another bolt of lightning flashed behind her. Startled, she dropped the ball of wind and it DRIFTED away.

"I think I can help you with this lightning," Paulina said.

"You've already said that," the fairy sneered.

"No, this is different," said Paulina. "I can show you how to CONTROL the power of the lightning, so the clouds will hold their charge."

"Really?" the two fairies asked together.

We all looked at Paulina, impressed. But, of course, she's a real SCIENCE WHIZ, so I wasn't surprised.

"I just need to do a small calculation," Paulina replied. "I will write it down for you, with one condition."

"What's that?" the fairies asked.

"That you let us PASS to the other side of the valley," replied Paulina.

"Do you know what you are asking?" the first fairy said. "That would mean **STOPPING** the Scarlet River, and we cannot."

"Never mind, then," Paulina replied.

The fairies flew toward each other and began to talk in whispers.

"Do you really know how to do that calculation?" Pam asked Paulina.

Paulina nodded. "I've never done it before, but I think I can."

"And what if something goes **wrong**?" Violet asked.

"I have faith in Paulina," Will said, and she smiled at the compliment.

A moment later, the two fairies flew back.

"We accept your proposal," said the first. "Too many of us have had trouble with lightning lately. But if your calculation does not work, you will not pass."

"That is fair," Paulina agreed.

"You will test this at the place where we gather THUNDERCLOUDS," the second fairy said, and the two fairies called down the wind again. They shaped it into a large sphere. It floated to Paulina and wrapped around her like a BIG BUBBLE.

I held my breath as I watched the bubble lift Paulina up higher and higher above us. She waved to us from inside.

"I hope that bubble doesn't BREAK," said Violet anxiously.

"These fairies might be cranky, but I think their magic is strong," said Nicky.

"I'm just impressed that Paulina can attempt such a difficult calculation," Colette said.

"That's the beauty of the THEA SISTERS," said Pam. "Each of us has a different talent. So no matter what situation we're up against, we can always succeed."

"At least, we hope so!" Nicky joked.

We all looked up at Paulina. The entire **MISSION** was riding on the shoulders of our **BRAVE** friend!

A WORLD OF COLOR!

While we waited for Paulina to return, we stared at the **Scarlet River** at the bottom of the valley.

"Look! *The river has stopped running!*" Nicky cried.

"Paulina did it!" Pam cheered.

A moment later the wind sphere **floated** back down to us, accompanied by the two fairies. Paulina was *smiling* as she stepped out of the sphere.

"I am so **PROUD** of you!" I cried, giving her a hug.

She smiled. "Thank you, Thea."

"**GOOD JOB!**" Will added, and Paulina beamed.

"How did you manage to figure out how to control the lightning?" Violet asked.

"I needed to create a **formula** to combine the velocity of the wind, the density of the clouds, and the power of the fairy dust," Paulina began, showing us the notes she had made.

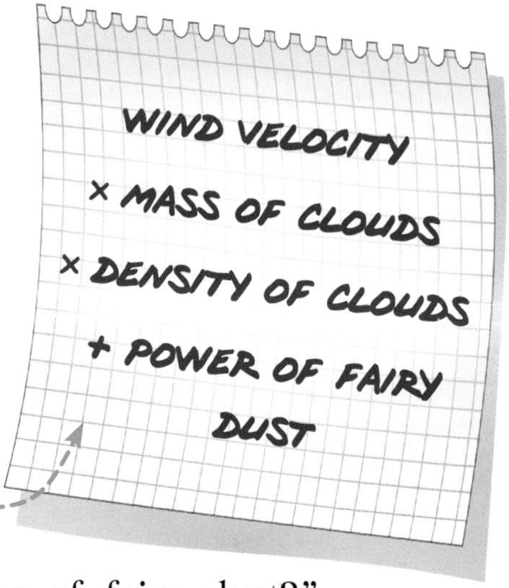

WIND VELOCITY
× MASS OF CLOUDS
× DENSITY OF CLOUDS
+ POWER OF FAIRY DUST

"How do you determine the power of fairy dust?" Violet asked. "It's a magical element."

Paulina nodded. "That's exactly why it was so **TRICKY**. But it has properties similar to —"

"**No need to explain!**" Colette interrupted, smiling. "We're just happy you did it!"

The Scarlet Lightning Fairies looked happy as well.

"We thank you," the first fairy said. "Now we can give the right amount of fairy dust to each cloud."

"And we won't get hit by lightning bolts anymore!" added the second.

"You will always be welcome in the Valley of Infinite Storm Clouds," the first fairy said.

The two fairies bowed. "Now you may pass."

"Can you point the WAY to Fairywing Village?" Will asked.

"Cross the valley and then go straight," the first fairy told him.

"Safe travels," said the second fairy. "We truly hope you can set things right in the Land of Clouds."

"We will do our best," Will promised.

We safely crossed the Scarlet River, climbed up the other side of the valley, and walked STRAIGHT AHEAD. We kept our eyes open for signs of Fairywing Village.

After a few minutes, I noticed something.

"I think I see a color cloud over there," I said, pointing. "Like the ones that marked the way before the Cloud Tunnel."

"I see it, too!" Colette said. "We're on the right path."

Soon, Fairywing Village came into view.

Look, color clouds!

FAIRYWING
VILLAGE

The pretty color clouds had little cloud houses on top of them in shades of PINK, YELLOW, GREEN, BLUE, and PURPLE.

"How cute!" Colette cried.

"But I don't see any pixies," Violet observed.

We looked around, hoping to spot someone who could help us, when Pam sneezed.

"ACHOOOOO!"

"Are you catching a cold?" Violet asked.

Before Pam could reply, we heard the sound of stifled giggles.

Then three pixies peeked out from behind a cloud and smiled at us. They fluttered their transparent wings and flew toward us.

The first was dressed in BLUE, the second in PINK, and the third in PURPLE. Each one carried a bucket of PAINT.

"Good day, Color Pixies," Colette said.

"Good day, dear," replied the blue pixie.

"We are Rosebud, Bluebell, and Lilac. Who are you?" asked the pink fairy.

We introduced ourselves, and Lilac frowned. "We do not allow strangers here."

"We have a **very important** reason for our visit . . ." I tried to explain.

Rosebud shook her head. "I'm sorry, we can't make any exceptions!"

Meanwhile, Lilac had begun to paint a cloud.

"You paint so well," Violet said. "May I try?"

"Certainly," said Lilac, and she handed the PAINTBRUSH to her.

Violet painted a **marvelous flower** on the delicate surface of the cloud.

"It's an orchid, my favorite flower," Violet explained.

"You are very good at **painting**," said Rosebud.

"Not as good as you, kind pixies," Violet said.

The fairies smiled at the compliment. "Thank you," said Bluebell. "We paint from sunrise to **sunset**, coloring the clouds."

They smiled again, and we remembered what Ariette had told us: if we made them laugh, they would let us enter the village.

"Would you like to hear a funny joke?" Nicky asked. "I know a good one."

The three fairies clapped their hands together. "Yes, please! Tell us a joke!"

"Okay," said Nicky. "What's worse than finding a worm in your **apple**?"

"I don't know. What?" asked Rosebud.

"Finding half a worm!" Nicky said, and the fairies giggled.

"Tell us another one!" said Bluebell.

"Okay," said Nicky. "What kind of fruit do twins like best?"

"What kind?" asked Bluebell.

"PEARS!" Nicky said, and the fairies giggled again.

"One more! One more!" pleaded Lilac.

Nicky thought. "Okay, here's a funny color riddle for you," she said. "A one-story house is painted PURPLE. The walls are PURPLE. The floors are PURPLE. The furniture is PURPLE. The ceilings are PURPLE. What color are the stairs?"

"PURPLE?" Lilac guessed.

Nicky grinned. "There are no stairs! It's a one-story house!"

The three fairies started laughing so hard that they somersaulted in the air.

"Your jokes have put us in such a GOOD MOOD," Rosebud announced.

"And when we are in a good mood, we like having guests for tea," Lilac added.

"Would you like to visit our homes?" Bluebell asked.

"We'd be delighted!" Will replied.

"Follow us!" Rosebud said.

We stepped along a path of color clouds, following the flying fairies.

"Good job, Nicky," I whispered to her. I was so PROUD of my student.

SMILE CAKES

As we walked through the village, we passed the **cute** little houses perched on color clouds. From their chimneys came the delicious **aroma** of desserts baking.

"What a wonderful place!" Violet said, looking around.

"Fairies of **all different colors** live in our village," Lilac explained. "Each one of us has a paintbrush and a palette that we use to **PAINT** the clouds."

The three fairies led us to a **pale blue** house that I guessed was Bluebell's.

"You are **lucky** to live in such a pretty village," Colette remarked.

Bluebell nodded. "Once, this was a very

happy place, full of laughter and joy," she said. "But now . . ."

"Now the clouds are **disappearing**, you mean?" Colette asked.

Bluebell looked surprised. "How do you know that?"

"That's the reason we came here. To solve this **mystery**," I replied.

The three fairies looked at one another, confused, but then Bluebell's eyes got wide.

"Goodness! My cupcakes!" she cried, and then she rushed into her house.

A moment later she flew back out. "I thought I had left them in the oven for too long! But they're perfect. Please, come in!"

In the center of Bluebell's tiny house was a round table laden with cupcakes.

"The smile cakes that Bluebell makes are famous throughout the village," Rosebud told us.

We took our seats around the table and each took a cupcake.

"These are delicious!" Pam exclaimed, biting into a chocolate cupcake decorated with colored sprinkles.

"I'm happy you like them," Bluebell said

with a satisfied smile. "Now that there aren't any new clouds to paint, we have to find other ways to keep busy."

"We're here to find out what is happening to the clouds," Will said. "We want to SOLVE the problem and save the land."

"But nobody knows how to make the Weaver Fairies dream again," Lilac pointed out.

"Well, maybe the reason that the Weaver Fairies aren't making silver thread isn't what you think," Colette suggested.

Lilac got annoyed. "Oh, really? Do you know better than Queen Nephele?"

"Well, not even she knows the real reason," Will said. "There is only one fairy who can truly find out."

"And who might that be?" Rosebud asked.

"Ariette, the Weaver Fairy," Will said.

The fairies' eyes widened.

"Ariette? She is the cause of all this **trouble**!" Lilac protested.

"But Ariette is the only one who can see the dreams of the Weaver Fairies," Paulina broke in. "Maybe the fairies are still

dreaming, but what they are dreaming is keeping them from weaving. We need to understand what is going on."

"Queen Nephele and the Grand Council of Fairies have established the GUILT of Ariette according to the law. There is nothing more to say," Bluebell said firmly.

"Please, Color Pixies, give us a chance to find out the truth," Violet pleaded. "If Ariette were free, she could —"

"Free?" Rosebud interrupted angrily. "It's out of the question. It would mean giving her back her CRYSTAL PENDANT."

"And we know you're guarding it here!" Pam blurted out.

Nicky nudged her, but it was too late. Our plan to sneak off with the crystal was exposed.

"So you're here to steal Ariette's crystal?!"

Bluebell asked **ANGRILY**.

Rosebud took out a silver whistle and blew into it three times. A moment later, we heard the strong beating of wings. We stepped outside and saw three majestic **winged unicorns**!

"They will take you to the Cloud Castle. **Queen Nephele** and the Grand Council of Fairies are waiting for you," said Lilac **STERNLY**.

Will turned to us. "We may as well go to the palace. We may get more information there."

We nodded in agreement, and then climbed onto the backs of the **unicorns**. They **soared** up high, whisking us away from Fairywing Village.

Good-bye!
How exciting!
I love unicorns!

INSIDE THE CLOUD CASTLE

I couldn't believe that we were flying on unicorns! It was amazing. Their long wings kept us steady even when heavy GUSTS OF WIND hit us. They rode the air currents, FLYING SWIFTLY toward the Cloud Castle.

"Do you think the Grand Council of Fairies will be angry with us?" Violet asked behind me.

"They might," I replied. "But I am counting on the wisdom of Queen Nephele. I hope that she will see the TRUTH once we explain our reasoning."

"And if she doesn't?" Violet asked.

"Then we'll have to think of a PLAN B," I replied. Though I didn't exactly know what that would be.

"**LOOK UP AHEAD!**" Colette shouted.

An enormouse palace came into view on the horizon: **the Cloud Castle!**

The unicorns landed in a large courtyard.

Seven guards in silver armor were lined up there, waiting for us. Two **winged fairies** stood in front of them. They were all looking at us severely.

"Welcome. We are the Sentinel Fairies, and these are the **Cloud Guards**," explained the fairy with long red hair. "Follow us, please."

The Cloud Guards led us inside the palace.

THE CLOUD CASTLE

1. Palace entrance
2. Fountain of Dreams
3. The Guards' Courtyard
4. The Fairies' Courtyard
5. The Queen's Courtyard
6. Throne Room
7. North Wing (royal quarters)
8. East Wing (Weaver Fairies' quarters)
9. South Wing (quarters for the Grand Council)
10. West Wing
11. Hall of Mirrors

6
7
11
4
1
3
8
2

Inside, we could see that the building was made of the woven threads of clouds.

"How elegant!" Colette exclaimed, looking at a fancy stuffed armchair.

"Those were just created today," said the fairy with dark hair, pointing to the chairs.

"What do you mean, 'created'?" Nicky asked.

"The cloud threads are soft and can be woven to create many different shapes," explained the red-haired fairy. "Therefore, the furniture of the castle is constantly CHANGING, to always keep it as beautiful as possible."

"And of course every fairy can change the FURNISHINGS of her own room as often as she wishes," added the dark-haired fairy.

"I would love to do that back in our room at Mouseford!" Colette said with a dreamy sigh.

"You would change things every day!" Violet teased.

We reached a very tall door with two LIGHTNING BOLTS carved on it.

The dark-haired fairy turned to us. "Wait

here," she instructed, and she went inside with her companion.

The Cloud Guards stayed behind with us. It was clear that they weren't going to let us out of their sight for a moment.

A few minutes passed, and the fairy with dark hair returned.

"You may enter," she said.

We found ourselves in a very GRAND HALL in the shape of a circle, with a row of benches around the room occupied by fairies. All of them wore dark blue dresses decorated with tiny crystals. On the throne, in the middle of the room, sat Queen Nephele. She wore a turquoise dress and a crown of stars on her head.

Hardly daring to breathe, we sat in seven seats facing the queen, waiting to be heard by the Grand Council of Fairies.

Welcome, strangers!
Thank you, Your Majesty!
It is an honor!

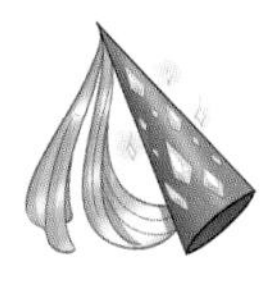

THE GRAND COUNCIL OF FAIRIES

Queen Nephele broke the **deep silence** in the council room.

"Welcome to the Cloud Castle, strangers," she said. "I am Nephele, Queen of the Land of Clouds, and this is the Grand Council of Fairies. I imagine that you know why you are here."

"It's an **honor** to be in your presence, Queen Nephele," Will said. "We are here to help you."

The queen looked at him questioningly. "What do you mean?"

A low murmur rose among the fairies in the council.

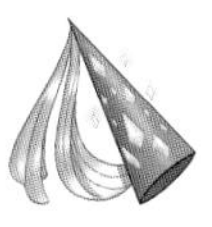

"We know that the Weaver Fairies aren't weaving any more clouds," Will said. "And we're here to find out why."

"You are late, strangers," the queen said. "The truth is already known. It was this very council that JUDGED the guilty party and took the necessary actions."

Ariette is guilty!

"If you're talking about Ariette, we've met her," I said.

Another murmur rose up.

"We went into her tower and spoke to her," Pam added confidently.

"She told us that she is innocent, and that she can FIND OUT the reason the fairies aren't

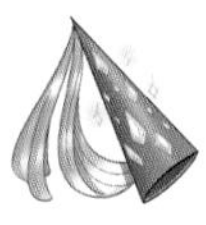

producing silver thread," Colette said.

"That's absurd!" fumed the queen. "She is guilty of describing the World Below to other fairies. That is against our LAW, and she was punished."

"But we come from the World Below, and it is full of wonders," Violet said.

The queen stared at us in SHOCK.

"Please FREE Ariette," Paulina pleaded. "Punishing her has not solved the problem of the Weaver Fairies. And she is the only one who may be able to learn the truth."

Queen Nephele shook her head. "No. Absolutely not. Ariette put our realm in SERIOUS DANGER and must stay in the tower. The Weaver Fairies will start weaving again soon, once they forget what she has told them."

The fairy council nodded in agreement. Only one fairy stood and bravely challenged the queen.

"My queen, I beg you. Listen to these strangers. They are telling the truth about Ariette," she said.

"Galatea! We have already discussed this at length. The decision has been made," Queen Nephele said.

Galatea lowered her gaze and sat down again.

My queen!

The queen continued. "I order that these strangers be taken to the castle library. They will stay there, under the custody of the Cloud Guards, while they wait to be removed from our land and returned to the WORLD BELOW. I hereby declare this meeting **OVER**."

The queen stood and left the

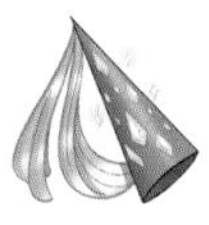

hall, and the council members followed her — except for Galatea. When the Cloud Guards approached us, she stopped them.

"I will accompany these strangers. Please go."

They left, and Galatea led us to the library.

"So, you have seen my friend Ariette?" she asked.

"Yes," said Will. "We were trying to find the Cloud Castle when we heard her cries from the tower."

"Poor Ariette," said the fairy. "I wish I could help her, but I don't know how."

"She told us she can't leave the tower without her CRYSTAL," Colette said.

Galatea nodded. "That is true. The crystal produces a magic

light that surrounds the fairy wearing it and allows her to move across the clouds."

"It sounds beautiful," said Colette.

Galatea grasped the PENDANT that she wore around her neck. "This is my crystal."

"It's so sparkly," Violet said admiringly.

"Why is it against your laws to explore the World Below?" Pam asked.

"The rcason is fear," Galatea replied. "Queen Nephele and many of the fairies don't know much about other worlds, and so they believe they must be dangerous."

"But that's not true," Paulina said, shaking her head. "It is a wonderful experience to get to know new people and places."

"I agree," Galatea said. "But I think it will be a long time before the Grand Council of Fairies understands that."

"That's a shame," said Colette.

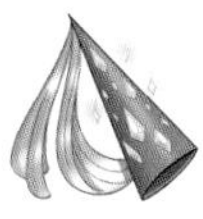

Galatea sighed. "Meanwhile, Ariette is a PRISONER. I'm so worried about her."

"Are you good friends?" Nicky asked.

"Yes. We are always together and share everything," Galatea replied. "I know it's not her fault that the Weaver Fairies are no longer producing silver thread."

"Do you have any clue why it's happening?" asked Will.

Galatea shook her head. "No. Ariette is the only one who can find out, if she can ever LEAVE that tower!"

"We tried to get her crystal back from the Color Pixies, but unfortunately we didn't succeed," I explained.

"There's another way to free Ariette," Galatea said. "But I can't do it alone. Would you be willing to help me?"

"**Absolutely!**" we all replied.

A GESTURE OF THE HEART

We entered the Cloud Castle's library and **Galatea** closed the door firmly behind us. We were alone.

"What is **YOUR PLAN**?" Will asked.

The fairy slipped off the chain around her neck and handed it to Will. It was her **CRYSTAL**.

"Why did you take it off?" he asked her.

"So that you can take it to Ariette, and she will finally be **FREE**," Galatea said.

"But I thought that each fairy had her own special crystal," said Will.

"That is true," Galatea said. "Each crystal represents the nature of the fairy who wears it, and it is very personal to her. But it can be given from one fairy to another."

"And it still maintains its MAGIC POWER?" Will asked.

Galatea nodded. "Yes."

Paulina looked worried. "But what will you do without your crystal?"

"I will stay confined here," Galatea replied. "I won't be able to fly or leave the Cloud Castle. But I will gladly do it, because it's the only way to help Ariette prove her **innocence**."

"What a nice thing to do," I commented.

"Ariette is my dear friend, and I love her very much," said Galatea. "It is unjust that she is a PRISONER in the tower."

We nodded in agreement.

"And it is important to find out what is happening with the Weaver Fairies," Galatea continued. "If they don't start weaving clouds again soon, the Land of Clouds will be in SERIOUS DANGER!"

"You're right. We'll take the pendant to Ariette and FREE her as soon as possible," Will said. He placed the pendant gently in Colette's paw. "The tower is far away and will take us a long time to reach," he continued. "Can you stay here long without your CRYSTAL?"

"The unicorns can take you to Ariette, and they are fast," Galatea reminded him.

I also still had one worry about the plan.

"I think it would be better if you didn't stay here alone," I told Galatea. "Without

the power of your crystal, you could be in DANGER."

"Especially if Queen Nephele finds out that you let us escape," Paulina said. "She might get ANGRY."

"Let's split up into **two groups**," Will said. "One will stay here at the castle with Galatea and try to make sure that Queen Nephele and the Grand Council do not suspect anything. The other group will go FREE Ariette, help her get back her CRYSTAL from Fairywing Village, and then bring her back to the palace."

"If you all agree," I proposed, "I will stay here at the palace with Pam and Violet."

Everyone was happy with that plan.

Before we separated, we **hugged** one another tightly. Then Colette, Nicky, Paulina, and Will flew away on the magic unicorns.

Bye!
We're off!
See you soon!
Safe travels!
Be careful!

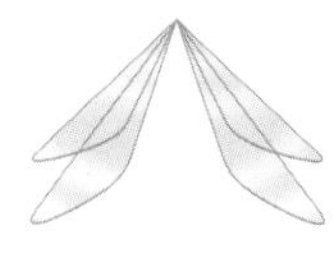

FINALLY FREE!

Will held on tightly to the unicorn's mane as they flew to Ariette's tower. He is a brave adventurer, but riding on the back of a unicorn made him nervous! Behind him, Paulina looked down on the Land of Clouds in wonder.

"There's Fairywing Village," she said. "And up ahead, I can see the Scarlet River!"

"It looks like a beautiful painting from up here!" Colette called out.

"I can see things that we didn't notice before," added Nicky, who was sitting in front of Colette. "There are cloud forests and cloud lakes down there, and all kinds of fairies!"

"It's like we're **flying through a dream**," Paulina said.

"Yes," agreed Will. "Fantasy worlds take us to **unforgettable** places. It's one of the reasons why I love my work!"

They continued in silence, **enchanted** by the beauty surrounding them, until they finally saw the tower where Ariette was held.

"At least we don't have to climb the tower this time," Colette said. "But how will we get inside?"

"Let's fly as close to the **WINDOW** as we can," Will suggested.

Ariette heard their voices and ran to the window. "You came back!" she said, greeting her new friends with a **brilliant smile**.

"We've come to get you out of here," Will told her.

"But the unicorns' wings won't let us get

any closer," Nicky pointed out.

Colette took Galatea's CRYSTAL from her pocket and looked at it thoughtfully.

"Try putting it on," Will said.

Colette's eyes widened. "Do you think it will make me FLY? But I'm not a fairy."

"It's worth a try," Nicky said.

Paulina turned to Will. "Do you think anything BAD could happen?"

"I don't think so," Will replied. "And we're ready to help if anything goes wrong."

After a pause, Colette put the CRYSTAL around her neck.

Immediately, she sensed a change inside her. She felt incredibly light . . .

"You're flying, Coco!" Paulina exclaimed.

"It's true! I can't believe it!" Colette cried as she floated off the unicorn's back. It felt amazing! But she had to focus on the job at hand: helping Ariette.

She FLEW through the open window, landing next to the fairy.

"How did you do that?" Ariette asked.

"Thanks to this," Colette said, showing her the PENDANT.

Ariette gasped. "But that's Galatea's crystal! Why do you have it? Did something happen to her?"

"No, she is fine," Colette promised. "We

met her in the Cloud Castle, and she gave us the CRYSTAL to bring to you."

Ariette's pale eyes filled with tears when she heard this.

"Ariette! Why are you crying?" Colette asked.

"Galatea has a heart of gold," she replied. "I don't know any other fairies who would have done the same."

"You are her best friend, and she would do anything to help you," Colette said. "It's thanks to her that we are here."

"But why would she give me her crystal?" Ariette asked.

"We weren't able to steal your CRYSTAL from the Color Pixies," Colette explained. "She knew this was the only way to FREE you."

Colette removed the necklace and handed

it to Ariette. The fairy put it around her neck, and it shone brightly. She happily flapped her wings.

"Let's go! Grab my hand!" Ariette told Colette.

Colette obeyed, and she felt a lightness flow through her body again. Then she and Ariette flew out through the window.

"You did it!" Nicky cried.

"Hooray!" cheered Paulina.

Colette climbed back onto the unicorn with

Nicky, while Ariette thanked the others.

"Now let's get back your crystal!" Will said.

"It's still at Fairywing Village," Paulina explained. "Things with the Color Pixies did not go well."

"Colette told me," Ariette said. "But I am not surprised. They are very stubborn."

"As soon as we mentioned the crystal, they called the unicorns with a silver whistle, and the unicorns took us to the Cloud Castle," Colette said.

Ariette nodded. "It's a good thing you met Galatea there and she gave you her crystal."

"And she helped us escape," Will added. "Some of our friends stayed with her, to protect her in case Queen Nephele suspects anything."

"You've done well," said Ariette. "If the

queen were to find out what Galatea did, she would be FURIOUS and would severely punish her. But there's another reason we should worry."

Paulina frowned. "What?"

"The exchange of crystals between fairies can be VERY RISKY," Ariette replied. "As you know, each crystal represents the nature of the fairy who possesses it. If a fairy goes too long without her pendant, she will lose her fairy powers forever."

"That's awful!" Colette exclaimed.

"It may already be TOO LATE for me. I do not know," Ariette said sadly. "But I do not want the same thing to happen to Galatea."

"Then we must HURRY!" Will said.

Ariette beat her wings and flew off to Fairywing Village, and our friends followed her on the unicorns.

A STORM OF STARS

As they flew toward Fairywing Village, the sky began to DARKEN.

"I wonder what time it is," Nicky said.

She looked at her watch, but the numbers on the face kept appearing and disappearing. This always happened in fantasy worlds: the technology of the real world stopped working.

"It will be NIGHT soon," Ariette confirmed. "And that's good for us, since it will be easier to avoid being seen."

Then Ariette let out a sigh.

"What is it?" Will asked her. "You seem worried."

"I am just sad that we have to steal the

crystal from the Color Pixies," she said. "They really are very sweet at heart."

"That's true," replied Will. "But we are only doing it to save the Land of Clouds."

"When it's all over, I'm sure the pixies will understand," Colette said. "After all, they'll have plenty of clouds to PAINT again!"

Suddenly, a small SHINING BALL fell from the sky and hit Paulina on the head. As soon as it touched her hair, the sphere dissolved into a spray of stars.

"Oh!" Paulina cried.

"What happened?" Will asked.

But before she could answer, a shining ball hit him, too!

"It's a storm of stars! We must find shelter!" Ariette cried.

The fairy dove for a low bank of clouds. The unicorns followed her.

"Quickly!" Ariette urged them.

Meanwhile, the STARS continued to fall, as thick as snowflakes during a blizzard.

Each time the stars hit something, they dissolved, leaving a shining trail. Luckily,

my friends reached the low clouds quickly.

Then Paulina realized something. "These aren't clouds . . . they're flowers!" she cried.

"Let's go down farther," said Ariette, pointing to some huge trumpet-shaped flowers. "They will give us cover."

"Are the flowers STRONG ENOUGH to withstand the star shower?" Will asked.

"Yes, but we must be very careful around them," Ariette said. "Some of these flowers

How strange . . .
These flowers will make us fall asleep!

may make us fall asleep," she explained. "We are in Sleep Flower Woods, home of the Sleep Fairies. Only they know which flowers cause sleep."

"The Sleep Fairies? What powers do they have?" Will asked.

"They collect pollen from certain flowers. Then they add the pollen to the evening clouds, and that pollen helps all of the fairies in our world fall asleep," Ariette explained.

"That is amazing," said Nicky.

"But dangerous for us," said Ariette. "This star storm will shake the pollen loose from these flowers. So we can't stay here for long."

As she spoke, a star hit the flower over their heads. They quickly ran to another nearby flower before the pollen could fall.

"I hope this star storm ends soon,"

Will said, worriedly.

But more stars STREAKED down from the sky, and very quickly another star hit the flower above them. They all ran for cover once more, but there wasn't a flower close by that would protect all of them. Nicky and Colette took cover together, Will and Ariette found a flower, and Paulina ducked under a pale blue flower.

ZAP! Another star hit it immediately, and before Paulina could run, grains of pollen showered her. Her eyes began to droop right away, and she slid to the ground like a rag doll.

"**OH NO! PAULINA!**" Will cried, racing to her side.

"She's falling asleep!" Colette said.

Paulina was resting in the big, curled leaf of the flower.

"**WE MUST WAKE HER**, quickly!" said Ariette.

At that moment, a **fairy** appeared from behind the flower stems. She was tall and slender, and wore a **large pink flower** hat on her head. She *smiled* silently.

THE LEGEND OF THE SLEEP FAIRIES

"Good evening, my dear guests," said the fairy in a voice as musical as a lullaby.

"Good evening to you, Sleep Fairy," Ariette replied.

"Oh, a Weaver Fairy in these woods. What a surprise!" the fairy marveled.

"We are in the middle of a difficult situation, Sleep Fairy," Ariette said. "Our friend Paulina breathed in pollen from this blue flower and now she has fallen asleep."

"Can you please help us wake her up?" Nicky asked.

The fairy shook her head. "I am sorry, but I can't."

"How long will she sleep for?" Colette asked.

"She will wake up by herself, after having dreamed and rested," the fairy replied.

"But we are on an important mission. We can't wait," Will said.

"I am sorry," said the fairy. "Your friend's sleep is VERY GOOD for her."

"But there must be *some* way to wake her!" Colette said.

The fairy smiled. "You can try."

Colette shook Paulina's shoulder. "Wake up!" she said loudly. "It's me, Colette. We have to go!"

But Paulina continued to sleep deeply.

Ariette looked up at the sky. "The star storm is passing. The way is clear to Fairywing Village. I'm afraid we must leave her here."

"We can't. I will stay with her," Colette said.

Maybe the fairy felt sorry for them, because then she said, "Actually, there may be one way to wake your friend."

"What's that?" Will asked.

"There is a legend," the fairy began. "One night, a beautiful fairy fell asleep under a blue flower just like this one. She didn't wake up the next day, or the next. When one

of her sisters realized she was missing, she went out to search for her and found her here, in the Sleep Flower Woods.

"The sister tried to wake her, but without success," the fairy went on. "So she called on a young elf, a close friend of her sister's. She asked him to wake her sleeping sister, and though the elf didn't know what to do, he agreed to try.

So he knelt next to the fairy and kissed her hand — and the fairy opened her eyes!"

"What a romantic story!" Colette said.

"It is a beautiful legend," said the Sleep Fairy, "and we believe that it may be based on truth, like all legends. Only a true and **pure affection** can awaken those fallen into a deep sleep."

"Yes, but how does that help us?" Ariette asked.

Colette and Nicky looked at each other and smiled.

"We might have an idea," Colette said.

"Maybe Will could try to re-create the legend," said Nicky.

Will **blushed**. "Me? I don't know if that will work."

"You're the closest thing we've got to an elf," Colette said. "And you have a STRONG

CONNECTION with Paulina."

Will nodded. "I'll try."

He knelt next to Paulina, picked up her paw, and gently kissed it. Nothing happened right away. But soon Paulina's eyelids began to flutter! Very slowly, she opened her

eyes. Will quickly **let go** of her paw.

"Hooray!" Nicky cheered.

Paulina yawned. "What happened to me?"

"You fell asleep," Ariette explained.

"A **deep**, **deep** sleep," Colette added.

"But now you're fine," Will concluded. "That's all that matters."

Paulina nodded. "Yes, I only remember that I was having a good dream."

Her friends smiled.

"We must go," Will urged them. Then he turned to the Sleep Fairy. "THANK YOU FROM THE BOTTOM OF MY HEART."

"It was nothing," the fairy said. "I only told you a story."

Will, Paulina, Nicky, and Colette mounted the unicorns again. Then Ariette flew ahead, and they followed her to Fairywing Village.

THE RAINBOW MOTHS

Illuminated by the evening light, Fairywing Village was even more enchanting than Will, Colette, Paulina, and Nicky had remembered. When they got near the first cloud houses, Ariette stopped.

"We must be careful," she warned. "To protect their village during the night, the Color Pixies ask the Rainbow Moths to help."

"Who are they?" asked Will.

"They are creatures that are able to hear the smallest noise. When they sense danger, they release a colorful substance in the sky to alert the fairies," Ariette explained.

"But if the fairies are sleeping, how do

they see the colors in the sky?" Paulina asked.

"The Color Pixies are very sensitive to the smell of color," Ariette explained. "Each color has its own smell, and it makes their noses itch and wakes them up."

"Then we cannot ALERT the Rainbow Moths. But you said that they have very good hearing. How will we sneak past them?" Colette asked.

"We won't," Ariette admitted. "The Rainbow Moths will see us at the village borders. As soon as we enter the village, we'll just have to hurry and get the crystal."

Paulina nodded. "Where is it exactly?"

"It's kept in the Color Theater, which holds every shade of color that exists." Ariette answered. "But to get there we must pass through the GUESS-THE-COLOR MAZE."

"Mazes are fun," Paulina remarked.

"This one is special," Ariette said. "To reach the theater, you must figure out which COLOR hallway to travel down. Each could lead to the theater — or to nowhere."

Nicky frowned. "That sounds puzzling."

"It's a little tricky," Ariette agreed. "When you step inside the theater, the walls are white. You must call out a COLOR of your choice, which will then appear."

"And what if it's the wrong choice?" Colette asked.

"Then we must TURN BACK and start at the beginning," the fairy answered.

"And how do we know which color to choose?" Paulina asked.

"You must trust your intuition," Ariette said. "The correct color is different each time."

How wonderful!
Ooh!

Here's the maze!

With the plan in place, Ariette and the others **flew** into the village. As soon as they crossed the border, the Rainbow Moths flew toward them, leaving **color streaks** in the sky as they went.

"What an amazing sight!" Paulina exclaimed.

"We could enjoy it more if we weren't in **DANGER**," Will said.

They landed in front of the **GUESS-THE-COLOR MAZE**. A rainbow arched over the entrance.

"It's too bad Violet isn't here," Colette said, thinking of her **ARTISTIC** friend. "She would love this!"

"We'll tell her all about it," Will promised.

As they climbed off their **unicorns**,

they saw that the sky above them was marbled with **COLOR**. They heard a great **beating** of wings as they entered the maze.

"The Color Pixies are awake!" cried Colette.

INSIDE THE MAZE

"Let's try to hurry!" Ariette said.

Will looked thoughtfully at the maze.

"What's your **FAVORITE COLOR**?" he asked the others.

"Mine is **PINK**!" Colette replied immediately.

"I like green, the color of nature," Nicky replied.

"I like **ORANGE**," said Paulina. "It's so bright and happy."

Ariette smiled. "I like silver, the color of the clouds."

"And I like **BLUE**," added Will.

"We can only choose

one color to start," the fairy reminded them.

"Then I'll try!" Colette said. "Pink is my color. It won't let me down."

She took a step forward. "**PINK!**" she cried.

The floor and the walls of the maze immediately turned Colette's favorite shade of bright pink.

"WOW! AMAZING!" she exclaimed. "I need to paint the walls of my room this color."

The others followed, trusting in her. They walked down a short hallway, which turned to the right. They walked down another hallway, and turned to the left.

"Are we turning in circles?" Colette wondered.

"Let's go a little farther," suggested Ariette.

The halls of the maze kept twisting and turning as they walked.

Finally, Nicky called out, "I see the theater! Colette chose the right color!"

"I knew that PINK would stay true for me," Colette said with a grin.

"I think the reason you succeeded is that you were so certain," Will said.

Tall columns marked the theater entrance, and another rainbow arched overhead.

There it is!
The theater!
We did it!

Will PUSHED on the door, but it wouldn't budge.

"We must hurry, before the Color Pixies find us," Ariette said anxiously.

They all tried the door, but it would not open.

"What do we do now?" Nicky asked.

Will turned to Ariette. "Is there ANOTHER way in?"

"This is the only door I know of," the fairy replied. "But let me fly and check."

Ariette flew off and

returned quickly, out of breath.

"I think I found something!" she said.

She led them around to the back of the theater. There was no door — only a group of NUMBERS painted on the wall.

"What could that be?" Colette wondered.

"I think it's a kind of puzzle," said Paulina, stepping up to closely examine the numbers. "It's connect the dots!"

She placed her paw on the number 1 and TRACED a line between that and number 2. Immediately, the imaginary line turned PINK.

"Keep going!" Nicky urged.

Colette glanced over her shoulder. "Are the Color Pixies close?" she asked.

"They must be," said Will, worried. "The moths would have awakened them all by now."

"But they must still pass through the maze," Ariette reminded him. "So we have a bit of a head start."

Will nodded. "That's good news."

As they talked, Paulina worked as FAST as she could to connect the numbers.

"It's taking shape," Nicky commented.

"Hurry, Paulina!" Colette urged.

They heard a flutter of wings overhead and looked up. The Rainbow Moths had made it through the maze!

"The Color Pixies can't be far behind," Ariette said.

Just then, Paulina CONNECTED the number 99 to 100.

"Done!" she announced with satisfaction.

Everyone admired the finished picture: it was the image of a beautiful fairy!

Then they heard creaking hinges.

"There must be a hidden door in the wall, and solving the puzzle has opened it!" Will realized.

The door swung open.

"Quickly now!" Ariette said, and they all hurried inside the Color Theater.

THE POWER OF FRIENDSHIP

Once through the door, they found themselves in a room full of marvelous COLORED LIGHT. The walls, made of clouds, constantly changed color.

"They remind me of THEATER LIGHTS," Paulina said, remembering the school plays at Mouseford Academy.

"It reminds me of a multicolored forest," said Nicky, looking around in awe.

Even Ariette seemed amazed. "I have never been inside here before," she said. "Others have described it to me, but words do not do it justice."

Will gazed around. There was so much to take in!

Where is the crystal?
Come with me!

"Do you know where we can find the CRYSTAL?" he asked.

"It is kept in the ROOM OF LIGHT," the fairy replied. "The pixies keep their most precious objects there. It is said to be the only room with a golden door. It should be easy to find."

And it was. They quickly located the GOLDEN DOOR, which was not LOCKED. When they opened it, they gasped in surprise as a flash of white light blinded them for a moment.

When their eyes adjusted, they saw the light REFLECTING over every surface.

"A crystal room! How gorgeous!" exclaimed Colette.

Looking around in wonder, they stepped inside. Ariette's crystal glittered on top of a pedestal of clouds in the center of the room. When she saw it, the fairy's eyes filled with tears.

Colette put a paw on her shoulder. "It must be wonderful to see it again."

Ariette nodded. "I just hope it is not too late and I still have my powers."

She reached out to take the crystal — and something blocked her hand.

"There is some sort of invisible barrier protecting the crystal," Ariette said.

Nicky tapped on it. "Should we try to break it?" she asked.

Will tapped on it, too. "It feels very hard, almost like GLASS," he said.

He pulled a small hammer out of his backpack and hit the barrier with it a few times, but it didn't BREAK.

"No luck," Will said with a frown.

"We have come all this way, and now we must give up," Ariette said sadly.

"We are NOT going to give up," Colette said firmly. "There must be some way to get past this invisible barrier."

She placed both paws on the barrier's TRANSPARENT SURFACE.

"Yes, there must be a way!" added Paulina, placing her paws next to Colette's.

Nicky walked up and joined her friends. Nothing happened for a few seconds, and

It's an invisible barrier!
What do we do?

then a SHINING FLASH burst from the crystal as if it were lit from within. A bright glow filled the room.

A moment later, the transparent dome DISSOLVED. Ariette took the crystal and stared at it in disbelief.

"I don't understand," said Nicky.

"We didn't do anything," added Paulina.

Ariette smiled at them. "You're wrong. You have done much, and my CRYSTAL knew that."

"What do you mean?" asked Colette.

"The heart on my pendant is sensitive to the strongest, purest feelings, like the friendship between you three," the fairy explained. "When it sensed your friendship, it responded with a burst of pure light."

Paulina looked surprised. "Then our friendship dissolved the BARRIER

protecting the crystal?"

"I believe so," replied Ariette. "It's clear that you love one another and **take care** of one another. And you transmitted all that to the crystal through your paws."

Colette, Nicky, and Paulina looked at one another and then all **hugged** tightly.

"FRIENDSHIP SAVES THE DAY!" they cheered happily.

"It's wonderful," said Ariette, thinking of her own dear friend as she looked down at Galatea's **CRYSTAL**, which still hung around her neck.

She slipped off Galatea's pendant and put it safely in her pocket. Then she put on her own crystal. Suddenly, her eyes became **bright**, her cheeks turned **PINK**, and her hair shone like **silk**.

Thank you, Galatea!

"I feel so much better," said Ariette.

"Do you still have your powers?" Paulina asked.

Ariette nodded. "I can feel them. But now I am worried about Galatea. We must return her CRYSTAL to her right away."

"But what about the Color Pixies? Won't they stop us?" Colette asked.

Ariette's eyes shone. "I have an idea. Follow me!"

ALL ABOARD!

As soon as they left the Color Theater, Ariette said, "I am a Weaver Fairy. Now I will weave something to let us leave this place."

Surprised, Will, Colette, Nicky, and Paulina watched as Ariette took an object from her pocket that looked almost like a KNITTING NEEDLE. Then she removed her shawl and unraveled the silver threads it was made from. She used the needle to weave a large fluffy cloud.

Ariette wove and wove without stopping, and the shining thread seemed like it might go on forever. But it did run out, and then Ariette began to shape the finished cloud with her hands. She made it into a

large hot-air balloon!

Finally she nodded to her new friends. "Everyone on board, quickly!"

Ariette flew alongside the balloon as the others climbed inside. Then she pushed it toward the wind, and the CURRENTS began carrying it away.

"We're flying!" Nicky exclaimed.

"But look down there!" Paulina cried.

The Color Pixies had caught up to them at last, along with the MAGIC UNICORNS.

"Unfortunately, there's not much wind," Ariette said. "If we keep going at this pace, they'll catch us. But I have another idea. They don't really want you — they want me and my crystal. I will lead them in another direction while you get back to Galatea."

"But they'll catch you!" Colette cried.

Ariette shook her head. "I am FASTER

This is great!
All aboard!

than the Color Pixies, and the magic unicorns are easily fooled. If I hide behind a cloud they will not find me."

Will nodded. "Good plan. **Be careful**."

"There's a strong air current above us that

will take you to the **Cloud Castle**," Ariette said. "I'll give you a push up there."

"Okay," said Will. "**Good luck!**"

With that, Ariette **flapped** her wings and gave them a **PUSH**. Will steered the balloon into the **air currents** as Ariette flew off, waving good-bye.

I will try to lose them!

QUEEN NEPHELE'S STORY

Back at the Cloud Castle, NIGHT had fallen.

"The fairies will all go to sleep now," Galatea whispered. "They retire early in hopes of having good dreams. Even if they aren't dreaming anymore."

You should rest . . .

"You look PALE," Violet noticed. "Are you feeling okay?"

"I'm a bit tired because I'm not wearing my crystal," Galatea admitted.

"Maybe you should rest," Violet suggested.

"No, I'll be fine,"

Galatea said. "Thank you. But I am worried about the rest of you. If Queen Nephele realizes that your friends have left the castle, there will be trouble."

"I think the fact that we stayed behind should confuse everyone, at least for a little while," I said. "And I am sure they will be here with Ariette soon. Then we can help them safely get to the quarters of the Weaver Fairies to figure out what is happening."

Galatea nodded. "Ariette should have the Dream Key with her. Unless . . . of course! When she was imprisoned, they would have taken the key from her."

"**What is the dream key?**" I asked.

"It opens the doors to the wing of the castle where the Weaver Fairies sleep," Galatea answered.

"Is there any other way to get a key to the Weaver Fairies' wing?" Pam asked.

Galatea nodded. "The queen keeps an extra key to each wing in her treasure chest inside a secret room in the Royal Wing."

"Can you take us there?" I asked.

"It won't be easy," Galatea said. "There is a hidden passageway that leads to the Treasure Room, but it's very difficult to find. And the chest is guarded by the crystal Eagles."

Violet shivered. "They sound beautiful but SCARY."

"They are both of those things," said Galatea. "They are TRANSPARENT creatures, capable of hiding anywhere."

"What do they do to intruders?" Pam asked.

"If you try to get past them, they will appear out of nowhere," Galatea said.

"Anyone who looks into their icy eyes will suffer a terrible fate. The eagles will steal their dreams so that they stop dreaming forever!"

Violet shivered. "That sounds AWFUL!"

Pam looked at me. "Should we try to get the key?"

"I think we must," I replied. "Without it, Ariette cannot get to the Weaver Fairies. But we must be very careful."

"Yes, the Crystal Eagles must be taken SERIOUSLY," Galatea said. "There is a legend about them, but I'll tell you on the way. We must hurry."

She led us down a long hallway full of windows facing the palace courtyard. It was dark outside, but the palace was shining, illuminated by brilliant crystals.

Galatea began the story in a low voice:

"Long ago, when Queen Nephele was just a **baby**, her parents were abducted by an **EVIL** wizard. The princess was so sad that she cried for days and days. From her tears were

born two TRANSPARENT Crystal Eagles. From then on, these MAJESTIC birds have watched over her and are always ready to protect her with their powers."

"What a sad story," said Violet.

"But it's also full of hope," I said. "At least something was born from her sadness."

"Maybe, but it would be better if the queen's parents could return one day," Violet said.

Galatea nodded. "Yes, Violet. We fairies hope for that each day, but unfortunately, nobody knows what happened to them."

"Maybe that's the reason the queen has such a stern personality," Pam guessed.

I thought Pam was right. "Often, a hard shell hides the sadness of a tender heart," I said.

Meanwhile, we had reached the end of the hallway. In front of us was a LONG STAIRCASE that led to the rooms of the fairies of the Grand Council. One floor above them were the queen's quarters.

THE TREASURE ROOM

"The Cloud Castle is filled with beautiful and interesting places," I remarked as we climbed up the staircase.

We reached a landing, and Galatea led us through a door at the top. It revealed a hallway lined with silver doors decorated with crystals.

"Those are the rooms of the fairies of the Grand Council," she explained.

"It almost looks like the dormitory at Mouseford!" Pam remarked.

"With a lot more BLING," Violet said, touching the door.

"The hidden passageway is on this floor, but we must pass through here quietly,"

Galatea whispered. "The fairies should all be asleep, but if anyone wakes and finds us here, there will be trouble."

We tiptoed down the hallway and turned down another one. The walls of this hall were made of purple clouds with white patterns on them. Crystal sconces LIT UP the walls.

"The door to the passageway is here, but it is invisible," Galatea told us. "If I had my crystal, I could find it more easily. But without it, I am not sure where to LOOK."

"So now what do we do?" asked Pam.

"We must carefully feel the wall," Galatea answered. "The door is invisible, but we should still be able to find the doorknob."

It was a long hallway, so we quickly got to work, running our paws over every surface of the cloud walls.

"**Cheese and crackers**, I just can't find it!" Pam said after we had been looking for a few minutes.

"I can't find anything, either," Violet said.

Galatea put a warning finger to her lips.

"Shhh. We must not **wake anyone**."

"Sorry," whispered the mouselets.

We quietly continued our search.

I carefully moved my paws up and down the walls. The doorknob had to be there somewhere! Then, at last, I felt something solid and ROUND beneath my paw.

It was smooth and cold.

I grasped it and turned it. Immediately, I heard a CLACK, and the invisible door swung open.

Behind me, I heard the others gasp in surprise. The wall had opened into a secret passageway!

"YOU DID IT!" cheered Violet.

"With a little patience and a little luck," I said with a smile.

I gazed through the door. There was a staircase just ahead, leading UPWARD.

Galatea grabbed my arm. "WAIT, I forgot to tell you something important. After we go through the door to the Treasure Room, we cannot pass through it again. Once we leave, we must exit through the HALL OF MIRRORS. It is a twisty corridor of mirrors that can create DANGEROUS ILLUSIONS."

The Hall of Mirrors is dangerous!

"What do you mean?" Violet asked.

"Some of the images that the mirrors REFLECT are not real," the fairy explained. "We Cloud Fairies know which are the fake images right away, because we are creatures of the sky, pure and clear. But it may not be so easy for you."

"Because we come from the WORLD BELOW?" I asked.

Galatea nodded. "Exactly, Thea."

Violet looked thoughtful. "I was in a house of mirrors at a carnival once," she said. "I couldn't tell which reflection was the real me, and it terrified me!"

"Those who are afraid will not make it

out of the Hall of Mirrors," Galatea warned.

Violet took a deep breath. "I will be **STRONG**. I can do it."

"I know you can, Violet!" Pam said, putting a paw on her shoulder.

"And we will be right there to **help you** through it," I promised her.

"Well then, are you ready?" Galatea asked.

Pam and Violet looked at me and **nodded** firmly.

"Good," Galatea said. "I'll go first."

Then we walked up the stairs and entered the **TREASURE ROOM**.

We did it!
Look!
We found the dream keys!

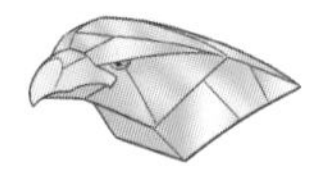

THE CRYSTAL EAGLES

The room that opened up before us was silent and illuminated by large CRYSTALS that resembled lanterns. As soon as we crossed the threshold, the door closed behind us, as Galatea had said it would.

"There are the DREAM KEYS!" Violet said, pointing to four keys hanging inside a case in the center of the room.

"We need the one for the East Wing, right?" Pam asked. "The Weaver Fairies' wing." She reached for the case.

"Don't forget, the Crystal Eagles may appear out of nowhere," Galatea reminded them, nervously glancing around. "And when they show themselves, don't look them in the

EYE, whatever you do."

I shuddered at the thought of having my dreams stolen from me. We had to get out of there quickly.

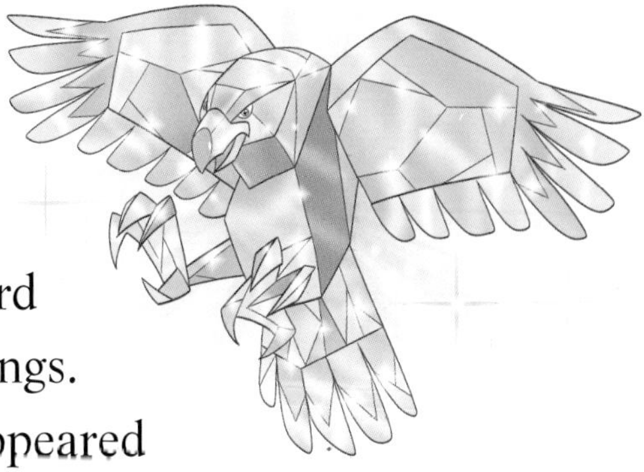

Suddenly, I heard a beating of wings. Then an eagle appeared in front of Galatea.

It looked like a GLASS SCULPTURE. It wasn't very big, but its shimmering wings sent flashes of light around the room.

Violet took a step toward me. Galatea remained still, lowering her head so she wouldn't look the eagle in the EYE.

"Noble eagle, allow us to take one of the dream keys," said the fairy.

The eagle beat its wings and circled the

room, then stopped again in front of Galatea.

"It's saying NO. It doesn't want to give us the key," Galatea said.

"Is there anything we can do?" asked Violet.

Suddenly, the second eagle appeared to us, sitting on its PERCH. It watched us, but we were careful not to meet its eyes. Even though I wasn't looking at it, I swore I could feel its gaze PIERCING right into me.

"Please, eagle friends. Give us the key we are asking for," said Galatea. "We must save the Land of Clouds."

The eagles beat their wings. Then the first flew back and joined the other on their perch.

"I'm afraid they won't change their minds," Galatea said sadly.

Then Pam made a **bold move**. She leaped for the case holding the keys. One of the eagles immediately took flight and swooped down, its **CLAWS** ready to grab her.

Before I could **HELP** Pam, Violet moved first. She jumped in front of Pam and stared the eagle right in the **EYES**!

For a second, all we heard was the beating of the eagle's wings. Then the bird returned to its perch, and both eagles disappeared from view.

I wasn't sure if Violet's courageous act had frightened the creature, or if the eagle had seen something in Violet's eyes — something that told it that we were on a NOBLE MISSION.

But Violet had met the eyes of the eagle. What would happen to her now?

Pam hugged her. "Violet! How do you feel?"

"I don't know," Violet replied. "My head feels strange. It's as if all my thoughts have been emptied. And I'm a little dizzy."

"Sit down a moment," Galatea said.

"Do you think the eagle has stolen her dreams?" I asked the fairy.

She nodded solemnly. "I'm afraid so."

"Oh, Violet! Why did you do it?" Pam asked her.

"Because the eagle was going to **ATTACK** you, and I couldn't let that happen," Violet answered.

Pam hugged her again, even more tightly this time. "You are the **best friend in the world**! Holey cheese! You'll get your dreams back, I promise you!"

"Don't worry, I'm okay," Violet said. "Let's get the key."

Galatea opened the case and took out a key with a handle in the shape of a spiraling whirlwind. "It's the key to the East Wing," she explained.

"We should leave right away," I said, and then turned to Violet. "Do you think you can keep going?"

"Yes, I can do it, Thea," Violet said bravely. "Whatever that eagle did to me, it didn't take my **STRENGTH**."

"This way," Galatea said, pointing to a door on the **left**.

"What about that one?" Pam asked, pointing to the door on the **right**.

"That one leads to the queen's quarters," the fairy replied.

"I'm surprised she didn't wake up," Pam said.

"She must be *dreaming*," said Galatea. "It's practically impossible to wake a Cloud Fairy once she's dreaming."

Then she looked sad. "Poor Weaver Fairies. I hope they get their dreams back soon."

"They will," I promised.

Galatea nodded. "But first, we must pass through the **HALL OF MIRRORS**!"

THE HALL OF MIRRORS

Before we entered the Hall of Mirrors, Galatea gave us some advice.

"LOOK carefully at each image you see in the mirror, and then ask your heart if it is rcal," she said. "That is the only way to get through this."

"We'll try," said Pam.

Galatea opened the door and we followed her into a narrow, twisting corridor completely covered in MIRRORS. Our reflections were multiplied dozens of times. Even though we had been prepared for this effect, we felt disoriented.

"Let's hold paws," I suggested, thinking this could help us.

We formed a LINE and proceeded down the hallway.

Galatea went first, followed by Violet, then Pam, and then me.

"Wow, there are a lot of Pams in here!" Pam exclaimed.

"I see myself everywhere, too," Violet said. "And I look so PALE."

"You're just a little tired," I said, but I was worried. Before we left the Land of Clouds, we would have to find a way to get Violet's dreams back. "Let's all try to stay calm," I said.

Galatea looked straight ahead as she led us. She seemed very FOCUSED on getting us through there as soon as possible.

"Hey!" Pam cried suddenly.

Violet spun around. "What's wrong?"

"I **bumped** my nose against my own reflection," she replied. Then she sighed. "I wish I had brought a **PIZZA** in here with me. I wouldn't mind seeing infinite pizzas!"

"How can you joke at a time like this?" asked Violet.

"Thea said to stay calm," Pam replied. "**JOKING** helps me stay calm. So does thinking about pizza."

Just then, I saw one of my **REFLECTIONS** staring at me. It looked like she was laughing at me!

I closed my eyes and opened them. This time, the reflection looked SERIOUS.

Violet must have had the same thing happen. "Thea, our reflections are PLAYING tricks on us!" she said.

"Yeah, my reflection just stuck her tongue out at me!" Pam said.

"Remember, they are only ILLUSIONS," Galatea said. "Don't let them upset you."

"Let's stop for a moment," I suggested.

We all stopped and took some deep breaths. Feeling calmer, we began walking again.

"How much farther do we have to go?" Pam asked the fairy. "It seems like this corridor will never end."

"That's part of the illusion," Galatea told her. "It's really not that far."

Then I saw something that made me **happy**. "Look! A door!"

Full of hope, I ran toward the door — and **bumped** right into it!

"It was just the **REFLECTION** of a door," Pam said, disappointed.

We looked around and realized there were **EIGHT** doors in front of us!

"Which door is the real door?" Pam asked.

Galatea studied them. "It is difficult to tell without my crystal, but I sense it is this second one."

She approached it — but that was just a mirror, too.

"SEVEN is my lucky number. Maybe it's the seventh one," Pam said, but she bumped into a reflection as well.

I took another deep breath and tried to concentrate. Galatea had told us to trust our hearts. And my heart told me to try door number FOUR.

I reached out and touched the door, hoping with all my being that I would touch a real doorknob. Then I felt the cold sphere and knew I was right.

"It's the real door!" I cried.

"Hooray!" cheered Pam.

Violet and Galatea smiled with relief. I

turned the knob and the door opened. We were outside the Hall of Mirrors and in a large corridor full of windows.

"Finally!" Pam exclaimed.

Pam rushed to an open window to get a breath of FRESH AIR. Then her eyes grew wide.

"**Great sticky pistons!** Look at that!" she said, pointing.

We rushed to her side. Through the window, we could see something flying down from the sky into the courtyard.

"It looks like a **hot-air balloon**," I remarked.

"It could be our friends returning!" Galatea said. "Hurry, follow me!"

She ***RACED*** down the corridor, and we took off after her.

FRIENDS REUNITED

We hurried outside and ran through the courtyards, toward the direction of the balloon. We all hoped the same thing: that Will, Nicky, Colette, and Paulina had returned with Ariette and her crystal. But the sight before us was **SURPRISING**.

Our friends were being carried by a hot-air balloon made of clouds! We had never seen anything like it. Ariette flew beside them.

"**You're back!**" Pam cheered as the balloon and Ariette landed.

The two fairies hugged tearfully.

"I am so **HAPPY** that you are back," Galatea said. "It must have been terrible to

You're back!
Will!
Hooray!

stay alone inside that tower!"

"It was very lonely, but I always knew that somehow I would escape and prove my **innocence**," Ariette said. "That helped me to get through it."

"I thought of you every day," Galatea said.

"Me, too, my friend. And thank you from the bottom of my heart for all that you did for me," Ariette said. Then she took something out of her pocket.

"My CRYSTAL!" cried Galatea.

"You saved my life," Ariette said, placing it around her friend's neck. Then she turned to the rest of us. "You all saved my life. How can I ever repay you?"

"There is no need," I said. "The greatest reward is to see you **FREE**."

"And to finish what we came here to do," Will said. "To save the Land of Clouds."

"Now Ariette can find out why the Weaver Fairies aren't making any more silver thread," Pam added.

"That won't be easy, I'm afraid," Ariette said. "I must enter the rooms of the Weaver Fairies, but the queen took the DREAM KEY from me when I was imprisoned."

"No problem," said Galatea. "We have ANOTHER ONE!"

Ariette was surprised. "How did you get it?"

"I took it from the queen's treasure chest," Galatea replied.

Ariette's eyes widened. "You went into the TREASURE ROOM? Without your crystal?"

"But I wasn't alone," Galatea said, looking at Pam, Violet, and me. We smiled.

"We managed to get through the HALL OF MIRRORS," Pam said proudly.

"You must have some story to tell us," Will said.

I glanced at Violet, noticing again how PALE she was. Now wasn't the time to tell that part of the story, though. First, we had to finish our task here.

"The Weaver Fairies are sleeping, so we should go to their rooms right away," Galatea urged. "Now is the perfect time to find out what is happening!"

Without another word, we slipped back into the palace again. Galatea and Ariette guided us silently through the corridors.

"It's so quiet," Colette said. "If the Weaver Fairies have been sleeping **soundly**, does that mean they're dreaming again?"

"Queen Nephele thinks the fairies might be having NIGHTMARES about the World Below, and that's why they're not producing silver thread," Ariette replied.

Then we arrived at the door to the East Wing. Ariette put the dream key in the **lock**. The door opened into a long corridor lined with the doors to the fairies' rooms, all slightly ajar.

"This way," whispered Ariette.

We FOLLOWED her, trying not to

make a **SOUND**.

Oddly, a **silver light** poured from each room. Ariette walked up to the first door. "***I can't believe it!***" she cried, shocked.

We all looked inside and **gasped**.

Look at that!
Ooh!

THE DREAMS OF THE FAIRIES

"It's silver thread!" Colette whispered excitedly. Next to each sleeping fairy's bed, a soft bundle of silver thread was forming.

"It is!" Ariette said happily. "I knew that the fairies hadn't stopped dreaming because of me."

Galatea squeezed her hand. "I was sure, too, my friend."

"But if the fairies are still producing silver thread, then what is the problem?" Paulina asked.

"That is what we need to find out," said Will.

We took a few steps into the room and looked around. The fairies slept calmly and peacefully. The only sound in the room was their light, rhythmic breathing.

Ariette approached one of the sleeping fairies. She closed her EYES and concentrated on the fairy's dream.

"What is she dreaming about?" asked Galatea, anxious to know.

"I see endless BLUE SKIES," Ariette reported. "She and her roommate are weaving baskets of clouds. And there are butterflies! Beautiful butterflies of every color, flying out of the baskets."

"But that's not a nightmare!" said Colette.

Galatea frowned. "And if the fairies are making silver thread, why aren't they WEAVING it into clouds in the morning?"

"It is strange," said Ariette. "The silver threads are always the first thing we see when we wake up. I did not see any in the tower, because I cannot make silver threads without my crystal."

"Let's check the other rooms," I suggested. "Maybe we'll find a clue."

Moving on tiptoe as quietly as possible, we went to the other rooms. We saw the same scene in each one: the fairies slept peacefully as bundles of silver thread grew beside them.

"This is a real mystery," said Pam.

Ariette suddenly held up her hand. "I thought I heard a noise."

"Maybe one of the fairies woke up," guessed Colette.

"Or maybe the queen knows we stole the dream key," Pam added worriedly.

Will walked to the door and looked up and down the hallway.

"I don't see or hear anything," Will said.

"Let's keep checking the rooms as *quietly* as we can."

We nodded in agreement and headed for the next room. Paulina stepped inside first, and we heard her gasp. We looked past her and our jaws dropped with **SURPRISE**.

A beautiful bird with **GOLDEN WINGS** was perched next to the bed of one of the fairies, and it was eating the silver thread!

"It can't be!" cried Ariette.

The bird heard her and raised its head.

It can't be!

"It's a SONGWING!" said Galatea.

"You recognize this bird?" Will asked.

"It is spoken of in the ancient legends of the Land of Clouds," Ariette replied. "The legends were often told to me when I was little and afraid of the dark. The story goes that the songwing came at night to help children sleep. It guided them toward good dreams with its golden wings."

"So it's a good creature," said Pam.

"Yes, of course I'm good!" the songwing piped up in a voice that sounded like the tones of a flute.

"Noble songwing, why are you eating our silver thread?" Ariette asked him.

"So that my wings can shine in the sky, kind fairy," replied the bird.

"But we need our silver thread to WEAVE the clouds," Galatea said. Without our

clouds, our land will disappear."

"I am sorry, but there is nothing I can do," the songwing said. "Lately the light in my feathers has **dimmed**. I am a mythical creature. I must shine BRIGHTLY to help the children!"

"But noble songwing, if you eat all of our silver thread, there will be no more children

to help," Ariette said sadly. "The Land of Clouds is in great DANGER!"

Suddenly, we heard **footsteps** in the corridor.

"It must be the queen!" Ariette said, alarmed. "We have been found out!"

And with those words, Queen Nephele swept into the room, accompanied by two fairies from the Grand Council.

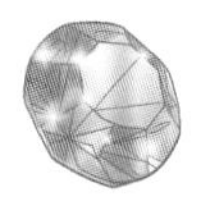

A GIFT FOR THE SONGWING

"Ariette!" exclaimed the queen. "How did you get here?"

Ariette bowed. "I ask your pardon, Your Royal Highness."

"There is no pardon for disobeying me," the queen said sternly. Then she noticed the rest of us. "What are they doing here?"

"Queen Nephele, please see what we have discovered," Galatea said, stepping aside to reveal the bird with the golden wings.

"A SONGWING!" the queen exclaimed in surprise.

"He is responsible for everything, Your Majesty," Galatea explained. "He eats the silver thread every NIGHT."

The queen was speechless for a moment, moving her gaze from the songwing to the bundle of silver on the nightstand.

"The fairies are still dreaming," she said. She turned to Ariette. "And you were telling the truth."

"Yes. I never lied to you," Ariette replied. "And I saw the dream of a sleeping fairy, and it was carefree and HAPPY."

The queen nodded, taking it all in. She put a hand on Ariette's shoulder.

"I owe you an apology, Ariette. The Grand Council and I inflicted an unjust punishment on you. For that I am truly sorry."

Ariette smiled. "The important thing now is that we have solved the problem."

Queen Nephele turned to the songwing. "You must LEAVE this place and stay away from our silver thread."

"Unfortunately, **I CANNOT**," the bird replied stubbornly.

The queen's eyes **darkened**, but Ariette spoke up. "I have a solution."

She took off her **CRYSTAL** and put it around the songwing's neck.

"Wear this, and your wings will shine in the sky like **TWO SUNS**," she said. "You will not need to eat our silver thread."

"Thank you, kind fairy!" he said.

"Now **fly away**, far from here!" Ariette told him.

The **mythical bird** took off out the open window, wings **SHINING**.

Colette gasped.

Good-bye, friends!

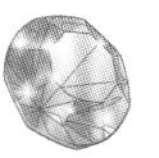

"Ariette, what will you do without your crystal? You will lose all of your powers — or worse!"

Ariette nodded. "I know," she said. "But I gave my crystal freely."

"You have such a big heart," Galatea said, her eyes filling with tears.

Queen Nephele looked at Ariette. "That was the crystal that you stole from the Color Theater, disobeying my orders."

Ariette lowered her eyes. "Yes."

"But you have proven your innocence, so I will pardon you," said the queen. "And not only that, you shall be rewarded for your generous heart."

The queen produced a small turquoise pouch and removed a PENDANT from it. She handed it to Ariette.

The fairy looked at it in disbelief. "This is

the Diamond Crystal! The brightest crystal in the realm."

"It is," said Queen Nephele. "And it belongs to the fairy with the purest, biggest heart. No fairy deserves this more than you."

Ariette put on the Diamond Crystal.

"It will be my TREASURE. Thank you, my queen," Ariette said, her eyes shining.

It's for you.

Thank you!

Queen Nephele turned to us. "Thank you, strangers, for all your HELP," she said. "I ask forgiveness for judging you wrongly."

And then she smiled for

the first time since we had met her.

"Your Majesty, there is something you can do for us," I began, and then I told her what had happened to **Violet**.

"Ariette, may I borrow the Diamond Crystal for a moment?" Queen Nephele asked, and Ariette gave it to her.

The queen held the PENDANT in front of Violet's face. Our friend closed her **EYES**. Then she opened them and smiled at us.

"I feel like myself again," Violet said.

"All is well," the queen reassured us, and she handed the pendant back to Ariette.

"Thank you from the bottom of my heart," I told the queen.

"We must celebrate!" the queen said. "Please stay and be our guests of honor in the Hall of Stars!"

THE GRAND CLOUD BALL

Inside the Cloud Castle, the Weaver Fairies made STAR decorations for the ceiling. They strung garlands of clouds made of glittering silver threads. As we admired their amazing skill, Ariette approached us.

"Do you like them?" she asked, pointing to the decorations.

"They're wonderful!" Colette replied. "Can you imagine if we had decorations like these at Mouseford Academy?"

"I've never seen anything like them," Will agreed.

"All the fairy creatures of the Land of Clouds and the neighboring realms will join the party," Ariette explained. "Now come with me. I want to show you something."

We followed her through the **corridors** of the castle until we reached the LIBRARY. On a large table in the middle of the room was a stack of shiny envelopes. Inside each was a lovely pink card.

"What elegant invitations!" Violet said.

"Would you help me **deliver them**?" Ariette asked us.

"OF COURSE we'll help!" we replied.

We followed her to the stables, where we found the flying UNICORNS. Then Ariette handed us silver thread.

"Hang the envelopes around the necks of

the unicorns," the fairy instructed. "They will **deliver** them."

As soon as every invitation was attached, the fairy gave a signal and the unicorns flew off. They were truly amazing, their glossy coats gleaming in the sun.

Galatea joined us. "The party begins soon," she informed us. "Queen Nephele asked me to take you to the fairies' wardrobe, where you can choose the dresses you would like to wear."

"Did you say *fairies' wardrobe*?" Colette repeated in disbelief. Then she looked at us with a twinkle in her eye. "**WHAT ARE WE WAITING FOR? LET'S GO GET READY!**"

The Thea Sisters burst into HAPPY LAUGHTER, and we hurried after Galatea.

"Let's not take too long," I said, thinking of Colette's usual behavior back at the academy. "We're the guests of honor. We can't be late!"

After we changed into our beautiful GOWNS, we entered the Hall of Stars. It looked magnificent! And each fairy wore a gorgeous dress in the color of a glowing jewel.

Ariette pointed to a group of princes across the room. "Those are the Princes of Nimbus, descendants of the ancient sky family," she explained. "They are known for their nobility

of SPIRIT and courage."

Then one of the princes broke off from the group and made his way to the queen.

"That's actually the King of Nimbus," Ariette said. "His name is Nebus."

Everyone bowed as he walked by. Then he greeted the queen with an elegant bow.

She gave him her hand and he led her to the center of the room, where the two began to dance with grace and elegance.

"They look made for each other," Nicky remarked.

"And they seem to be in love," said Violet with a smile.

Then the Princes of Nimbus approached our little group. Some invited the Thea Sisters to dance, while some stopped to talk to me and Will about their travels in faraway places.

How exciting!

You dance beautifully!

ALL THE COLORS OF THE CLOUDS

The party in the Hall of Stars was truly unforgettable. But when it ended, it was time for us to return home.

We all changed back into our regular clothes and got ready to leave.

"What a shame that we must leave the Land of Clouds so soon," said Violet when it was time to say good-bye.

"I will be sorry to see you go," said Ariette. "There are still so many things for you to discover here."

"We will never forget you," I said.

"Perhaps this will help you remember," a Color Pixie piped up. They had become friendly to us again after we were pardoned by the queen.

The pixie handed a box to Violet. She opened it to see **pots of paint** in every color.

"You can bring some of the **colors** of our world to the World Below," said Ariette.

"What a fantastic gift! Thank you!" said Violet.

"It's the least we can do to say thank you," said Queen Nephele.

"Thank you, Your Highness," said Will with a bow. "We must ask you for one last favor. We need to reach the **secret passage** to return home from the Land of Clouds. Can you show us the way?"

"We'll do it!" the Color Pixies offered.

Ariette and Galatea hugged us **good-bye**, and we bade our farewells. Then we climbed aboard some **fluffy** lilac clouds.

The Color Pixies led us to the silver gates where we had entered the **Land of Clouds**.

"We must leave you here," the pixies said. "Good luck!"

We waved to them and climbed off our **clouds**. We walked along a footpath of clouds until a light fog rose up around us.

We held paws and continued along the path. We weren't worried, though. By now

we were used to the feel of the clouds under our feet.

After a few minutes, the fog lifted.

"It's snowing!" Nicky cried.

"And look . . . we're wearing our mountain-climbing gear again," Colette said, looking down at her boots. "How can that be?"

Will searched the horizon for a landmark. "Those lights over there look like they could belong to our helicopter."

"Does that mean we're at base camp in Mount Everest, back in the real world?" Paulina asked.

Will smiled. "Journeys to fantasy worlds are always full of surprises!"

I nodded in agreement. And this time, the surprise was a good one. Our return to the real world had been so simple and sweet, like waking up from a wonderful dream!

ONE LAST SURPRISE

We were silent on the ride back to the **SEVEN ROSES UNIT**. Each of us was thinking about the EXTRAORDINARY adventure we had just experienced.

After the helicopter landed, Will turned to us.

"Once again, we have succeeded in returning **peace** to one of the fantasy worlds," he said. "Thanks to all of you."

"It was a demanding

mission, but we are always happy to help," I said.

"I could not have completed this **MISSION** without every one of you," Will said. "I'm sure the Seven Roses Unit will call on you again soon."

We said good-bye to Will and boarded the copter again for our return to Mouseford Academy. When we finally arrived, we were **happy** and excited, but also very tired.

I headed to my office to begin jotting down notes about the journey so I wouldn't forget. A few hours later, Colette and Pam **KNOCKED** on my door.

"Thea, could you please come to our room for a moment?" Colette asked. "We'd like to show you something."

"Sure," I said, feeling **curious**. "What's this about?"

Surprise!
Look at all the colors!
Wow!

"We can't tell you. It's a **SURPRISE**," Pam replied.

When I got to Colette and Pam's room, the surprise hit me with a **blast of color**.

The Thea Sisters had used the **pixie colors** to paint clouds all over the walls! I knew that those beautiful colors would always remind us of our journey through the **Land of Clouds**.

"This adventure was so amazing," said Paulina. "I can't even imagine what our next one will be."

Nicky smiled. "Well, I know that whatever happens . . .

OUR FRIENDSHIP WILL LEAD US TO SUCCEED!"

Don't miss any of my fabumouse special editions!

THE JOURNEY TO ATLANTIS

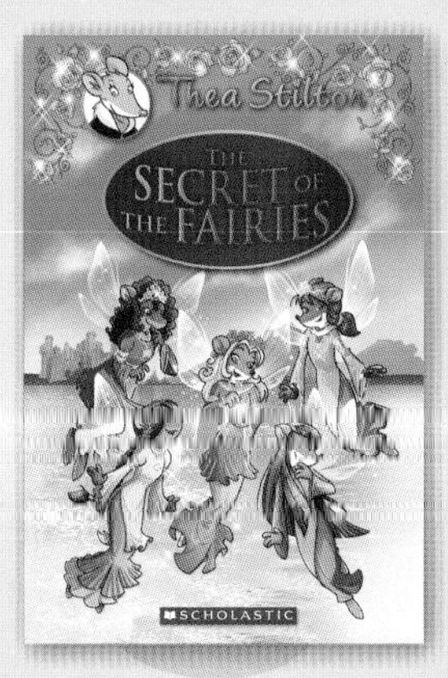

THE SECRET OF THE FAIRIES

THE SECRET OF THE SNOW

THE CLOUD CASTLE

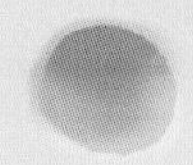

Don't miss any of these exciting Thea Sisters adventures!

Thea Stilton and the Dragon's Code

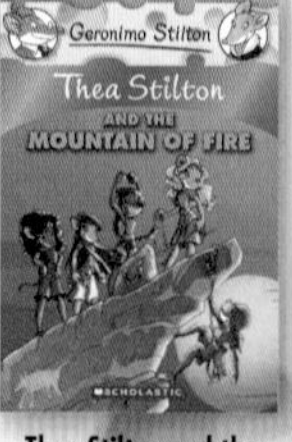

Thea Stilton and the Mountain of Fire

Thea Stilton and the Ghost of the Shipwreck

Thea Stilton and the Secret City

Thea Stilton and the Mystery in Paris

Thea Stilton and the Cherry Blossom Adventure

Thea Stilton and the Star Castaways

Thea Stilton: Big Trouble in the Big Apple

Thea Stilton and the Ice Treasure

Thea Stilton and the Secret of the Old Castle

Thea Stilton and the Blue Scarab Hunt

Thea Stilton and the Prince's Emerald

Thea Stilton and the Mystery on the Orient Express

Thea Stilton and the Dancing Shadows

Thea Stilton and the Legend of the Fire Flowers

Thea Stilton and the Spanish Dance Mission

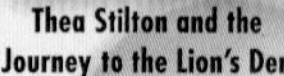

Thea Stilton and the Journey to the Lion's Den

Thea Stilton and the Great Tulip Heist

Thea Stilton and the Chocolate Sabotage

Thea Stilton and the Missing Myth

Thea Stilton and the Lost Letters

Thea Stilton and the Tropical Treasure

Be sure
to read all
my adventures
in the Kingdom
of Fantasy!

THE KINGDOM OF FANTASY

THE QUEST FOR PARADISE:
THE RETURN TO THE KINGDOM OF FANTASY

THE AMAZING VOYAGE:
THE THIRD ADVENTURE IN THE KINGDOM OF FANTASY

THE DRAGON PROPHECY:
THE FOURTH ADVENTURE IN THE KINGDOM OF FANTASY

THE VOLCANO OF FIRE:
THE FIFTH ADVENTURE IN THE KINGDOM OF FANTASY

THE SEARCH FOR TREASURE:
THE SIXTH ADVENTURE IN THE KINGDOM OF FANTASY

THE ENCHANTED CHARMS:
THE SEVENTH ADVENTURE IN THE KINGDOM OF FANTASY

THE PHOENIX OF DESTINY:
AN EPIC KINGDOM OF FANTASY ADVENTURE

Be sure to read all my fabumouse adventures!

#1 Lost Treasure of the Emerald Eye

#2 The Curse of the Cheese Pyramid

#3 Cat and Mouse in a Haunted House

#4 I'm Too Fond of My Fur!

#5 Four Mice Deep in the Jungle

#6 Paws Off, Cheddarface!

#7 Red Pizzas for a Blue Count

#8 Attack of the Bandit Cats

#9 A Fabumouse Vacation for Geronimo

#10 All Because of a Cup of Coffee

#11 It's Halloween, You 'Fraidy Mouse!

#12 Merry Christmas, Geronimo!

#13 The Phantom of the Subway

#14 The Temple of the Ruby of Fire

#15 The Mona Mousa Code

#16 A Cheese-Colored Camper

#17 Watch Your Whiskers, Stilton!

#18 Shipwreck on the Pirate Islands

#19 My Name Is Stilton, Geronimo Stilton

#20 Surf's Up, Geronimo!

#21 The Wild, Wild West

#22 The Secret of Cacklefur Castle

A Christmas Tale

#23 Valentine's Day Disaster

#24 Field Trip to Niagara Falls

#25 The Search for Sunken Treasure

#26 The Mummy with No Name

#27 The Christmas Toy Factory

#28 Wedding Crasher

#29 Down and Out Down Under

#30 The Mouse Island Marathon

#31 The Mysterious Cheese Thief

Christmas Catastrophe

#32 Valley of the Giant Skeletons

#33 Geronimo and the Gold Medal Mystery

#34 Geronimo Stilton, Secret Agent

#35 A Very Merry Christmas

#36 Geronimo's Valentine

#37 The Race Across America

#38 A Fabumouse School Adventure

#39 Singing Sensation

#40 The Karate Mouse

#41 Mighty Mount Kilimanjaro

#42 The Peculiar Pumpkin Thief

#43 I'm Not a Supermouse!

#44 The Giant Diamond Robbery
#45 Save the White Whale!
#46 The Haunted Castle
#47 Run for the Hills, Geronimo!
#48 The Mystery in Venice
#49 The Way of the Samurai
#50 This Hotel Is Haunted!
#51 The Enormouse Pearl Heist
#52 Mouse in Space!
#53 Rumble in the Jungle
#54 Get into Gear, Stilton!
#55 The Golden Statue Plot
#56 Flight of the Red Bandit
Special Edition!
The Hunt for the Golden Book
#57 The Stinky Cheese Vacation
#58 The Super Chef Contest
#59 Welcome to Moldy Manor
Special Edition!
The Hunt for the Curious Cheese
#60 The Treasure of Easter Island
#61 Mouse House Hunter
#62 Mouse Overboard!
Don't miss my journeys through time!
The Journey Through Time
The Second Journey Through Time